Giovan Gualberto Bottarelli

Il tutore e la pupilla, o sia Il matrimonio alla moda. The guardian and the ward; or Marriagealamode. A burletta. To be represented at the King's Theatre in the HayMarket

Giovan Gualberto Bottarelli

Il tutore e la pupilla, o sia Il matrimonio alla moda. The guardian and the ward; or Marriagealamode. A burletta. To be represented at the King's Theatre in the HayMarket

ISBN/EAN: 9783741183218

Manufactured in Europe, USA, Canada, Australia, Japa

Cover: Foto ©Andreas Hilbeck / pixelio.de

Manufactured and distributed by brebook publishing software (www.brebook.com)

Giovan Gualberto Bottarelli

Il tutore e la pupilla, o sia Il matrimonio alla moda. The guardian and the ward; or Marriagealamode. A burletta. To be represented at the King's Theatre in the HayMarket

Il TUTORE

E

LA PUPILLA,

O fia

Il MATRIMONIO alla moda.

THE

GUARDIAN

AND

THE WARD;

OR

MARRIAGE-A-La-MODE.

A BURLETTA.

To be reprefented at the KING's Theatre in
the Hay-Market.

LONDON:
Printed for G. WOODFALL, at Charing-Crofs.
1762.
[Price One Shilling.]

PERSONAGGI.

PARTI SERIE.

Rosmira, Figlia di Pasca-
sio, destinata Sposa di
Don Sabbione, amante
di Lindoro,
*La Signora Giovanna
Carmignani.*

Lindoro, Giovine Cava-
liere, amante di Ros-
mira, finto discepolo
di Contrappunto,
*Il Signor Giuseppe
Giustinelli.*

PARTI COMICHE.

Pascasio, Padre di Rosmira, Tutore, ed a-
mante di Timitilla,
*Il Signor Giovan Bat-
tista Zingoni.*
Timitilla, Pupilla in casa
di Pascasio, amante di
Don Sabbione,
*La Signora Anna Lu-
cia de Amicis.*
Don Sabbione, Marchese
di Scaccia pensieri, a-
mante di Timitilla,
*Il Signor Domenico
de Amicis.*

Parti di MEZZO CARAT-
TERE.

Contrappunto, Maestro di
musica, amante di Ser-
pilla,
*Il Signor Gaetano
Quilici.*
Serpilla, Cameriera di
Rosmira, amante di
Contrappunto,
*La Signora Marian-
na Valsecchi.*

Ballerini Principali.

Il Signor Gallini,
Mademoiselle Allelin,

Il Signor Binetti,
La Signora Binetti.

La musica è di varj celebri Autori, eseguita sotto
la direzione del Signor Giovanni Bach, maestro
di Cappella Saffone.

La Poesia è di Giovan Gualberto Bottarelli, all'
eccezione della quinta e dell'ottava scena del
terzo atto, e della maggior parte delle arie.

Dramatis Personæ.

SERIOUS CHARACTERS.

Rosmira, *Daughter to Pascasio, the designed wife of D. Sabbione, in love with Lindoro,* Signora Giovanna Carmignani.

Lindoro, *A young gentleman in love with Rosmira, a pretended scholar of Contrappunto,* Signor Giuseppe Giuslinelli.

COMIC CHARACTERS.

Pascasio, *Father to Rosmira, guardian to, and in love with Timitilla,* Signor Giovan Battista Zingoni.

Timitilla, *Ward to Pascasio, in love with Don Sabbione,* Signora Anna Lucia de Amicis.

Don Sabbione, *in love with Timitilla,* Signor Domenico de Amicis.

MIDDLE CHARACTERS.

Contrappunto, *master in love pilla,* Signor G lici.

Serpilla, *R in love punto,* Signo Vali

Principal Dancers.

Signor Gallini, Mademoiselle Asselin.

Signor Binetti, Signora Binetti.

The music is selected from various celebrated thors, and performed under the direction of John Bach, a Saxon master of music.

The poetry is by Signor Giovan Gualberto Bottarelli, except the 5th and 8th scenes in the third act, and the greatest part of the airs.

·A C T I.

S C E N E I.

hall in Pafcafio's houfe, with a harpficord and
chairs,

npunto at the Harpficord, Serpilla ftanding
Rofmira and Lindoro fitting with mufic-
1 their hands; afterwards Pafcafio.

MAY the newly married live
An hundred and an hundred years.

*How you fing that? What? can't you
Come, fafter.*

ay the newly married live
n hundred and an hundred years.

*, firs, a little flower, La, fa, mi, fol.
et's begin again.*

May the newly married live
An hundred and an hundred years,
Free from care,
And free from pain.

*`on. What difcord! juft like a parcel of cats a mew-
ing. Let's go on to the ducts.*

Serp.

ATTO I.

SCENA I.

Sala in casa di Pascasio con Cembalo e sedie.

Contrappunto al Cembalo ; Serpilla in piedi, da un lato del Cembalo. Rosmira e Lindoro a sedere con carte di musica in mano. Indi Pascasio.

Tutti. **V**IVAN gli sposi
  Cento anni, e cento————

Con. Zitti! che modo di cantare è questo?
  Non conoscete il tempo? Andiam più presto.

Tutti. *Vivan gli sposi*
  Cento anni, e cento————

Con. Piano, padroni. Adagio un poco più.
  Lai, lai, laran. Ricominciamo, sù.

Tutti. *Vivan gli sposi*
  Cento anni, e cento,
  Senza tormento,
  Senza dolor.

Con. Che confusion! mi pare
  Di sentir sgnavolare,
  Come se foste voi tanti gattini.
  Passiamo a' duettini,

Ser.

Ser. ⎱ *Sentir ſi dire*
Con. ⎰ *E ſpoſo e ſpoſa,*
        Che bella coſa !
        Che bel piacer !

Con. Brava ! Adeſſo a voi due ;
     Faccia bene ciaſcun le parti ſue.

Roſ. ⎱ *Dal Ciel la pace*
Lin. ⎰ *La gioia ſcenda,*
        E lieto renda
        Per noi tal dì.

Con. Avanti. Ser. Eh ! baſta, baſta. [*s'alzano.*
     Laſciamo queſta ſolfa. Lin. 'E vero : uniti
     Parliam di quel che preme, o fiam ſpediti.
Roſ. Oggi Paſcaſio vuole
     Spoſarmi a Don Sabbione. Con. In tre parole :
     Non—gli— riuſcirà. Roſ. Ma Come ? Con.
        Il come,
     Quando tempo verrà, ve 'l ſpiegherò.
     Farete a modo mio ? Roſ. V' obbidirò.
Con. Per or del voſtro padre alla propoſta
     Riſpondete di nò con faccia toſta:
     E voi Lindoro caro,
     Seguitate a paſſar per mio ſcolaro.
Ser. D' incanto ! Ma biſogna a Timicilla
     Tagliar le gambe, e preſto. Con. Ho già
        penſato.
     Nò, non mi ſon ſcordato,
     Quando mi ſtrappazzò,
     E maeſtro da dozzina mi chiamò.

Ser. ⎱
Con. ⎰   The endearing names
Of Bride, and Bridegroom;
How very charming!
How great a pleafure!

Con. *Very well. Now do you two begin, and each of you mind your part.*

Rof. ⎱
Lin. ⎰   From heaven, let peace
And joy defcend,
And fill this day
With happinefs.

Con. *Go on.* Ser. *Ab, enough, enough.* (They rife.)
Let's quit this finging.

Lin. *True; let's talk together of our prefent critical affairs, or we are undone.*

Rof. *This very day Pafcafio defigns to marry me to Don Sabbione.*

Con. *In three words. He—fhan't——fucceed.*

Rof. *But how fhall we binder it?*

Con. *The how I will explain to you at a proper time. Will you do as I direct you?* Rof. *I will be guided by you.*

Con. *For the prefent do you give a flat negative to the propofal of your father with a bold front; and you, dear Lindoro, continue to pafs for my fcholar.*

Ser. *Admirable! But we muft take Mrs. Timitilla a peg lower, and that very foon.*

Con. *I have contrived it; for I have not forgot her abufing me, and calling me paultry mafter.*

Ser. *You are worth the Indies.*

Con. *All we have to do is to ftick by one another.*

Rof. *I will do my part.*   2

Lin. *And I will lend a helping hand.*

Ser. *And I, to have my share in the action, will turn the house upside down: And if I have no other weapons to distinguish me, I can boast that I am not badly furnished with tongue.*

Lin. *The old man is listening.*

Con. *Come, on with you, begin the chorus again.*

                         [All resume their places.

Chor.   May the newly married live
              An hundred and an hundred years,
              Free from care,
              And free from pain.

Pas. *O what charming music! Health and prosperity attend the composer.*

Con. *I am Contrappunto, I know how to sing and compose correctly, and elegantly.*

Pas. *I am very sensible of it.*

Con. *We have not done : with your leave we will go on.*

Pas. *No, it don't signify. I want to speak just half a word with my daughter in private : You may come back again to sing an hour hence.*

Ser. *Must I go too ?*

Pas. *Yes, Serpilla.*

Ser. *Your servant (you know what is in agitation.)*

                      [To Rosmira, and exit.

Pas. *Excuse my freedom.*

Con. *Sir, We take our leaves.*

             [Contrappunto and Lindoro exeunt.

Pas. *This, my child, is the time for mirth——— This very day you shall be espoused to Don Sabbione— What a fine charming thing !—He will be here to see you in a very little time.*

                                  Ros.

Ser. Voi valete un Perù. *Con.* Solo dubbiamo
    Aiutarci un coll' altro. *Rof.* Io lo farò.
Lin. Ed io da buono amico opererò.
Ser. Io poi per farle guerra ; fottofopra
    La cafa volterò ;
od   E fe altra arma non ho, che mi diftingua,
    Mi vanto che ftò ben, ma ben, di lingua.
Lin. Zitti, chè il vecchio afcolta.
Con. Sù, via ; da capo, al coro un' altra volta.
              [*Tornano tutti al loro pofto.*

Tutti.   *Vivan gli fpofi*
          Cento anni, e cento,
          Senza tormento,
          Senza dolor.

Paf. Oh, che mufica bella !
    Viva il fignor maeftro di cappella !
Con. Contrappunto fono io. Bene, & pulito
    Sò cantare e comporre. *Paf.* ho già fentito.
Con. Non abbiam terminato. In grazia voftra
    Voglio che feguitiamo. *Paf.* Eh, non im-
    porta.
    Vorrei con mia figliuola
    Due paroline dir da folo a fola.
    Tornate pur a ricantar frà un' ora.
Ser. Devo partire io ancora ? *Paf.* Sì, Serpilla.
Ser. Serva. [*Sapete già quel che fi ftilla.*
                [*A Rofmira, e parte.*
Paf. Scufin la confidenza.
Con. Padrone ! Gli facciam la riverenza.
         [*Contrappunto, e Lindoro partono.*
Paf. Adeffo, figlia mia,
    E tempo d' allegria—
    Oggi di Don Sabbion farai la fpofa—
    Che cara e bella cofa !—
    Tra poco egli ti vuole vifitare.

ā   **B**   *Rof.*

Rof. Si potrebbe per oggi difpenfare.
Paf. Perchè? *Rof.* Perchè prevedo
Che ci faran de' guai.
Paf. Quefto difcorfo tuo mi fpiace affai.
Rof. Poffo fcoprirvi il cor libero & fchietto?
Paf. Sibbene. *Rof.* Non lo voglio. Il tutto ho
detto.
Paf. come! parli così col genitore?
Rof. Parla così chi non ha doppio il core.

> *Tutti i penfieri miei*
> *D' affetto, e di timor,*
> *Mio caro genitor,*
> *Noti vi fono.*

SCENA II.

Pafcafio, indi Timitilla.

Paf. Che modo di parlar! Oh, quefta è bella!
Son padre, e ubbidirà. Che sfacciatella!
Oh, oh, vien Timitilla,
La mia cara pupilla! Oh, che bruciore
Alla vifta di lei fento nel core!
Ma voglio darle loco,
E gli andamenti fuoi fpiare un poco.
[*Và in difparte.*

T.i > *Donne belle, miei Signori,*
> *Ecco quà la Timitilla.*
> *Son pupilla, giovinetta,*
> *Semplicetta, modeftina.*
> *Non fon fina, non accorta.*
> *Sol m' importa il voftro affetto,*

Rof. I could dispense with his attendance to-day.

Paf. Why so?

Rof. Because I foresee some inconveniencies.

Paf. This discourse of yours is very displeasing to me.

Rof. Shall I lay open to you my whole heart?

Paf. Yes, do.

Rof. I will not have him. I have said all I have to say.

Paf. How? Do you talk thus to your father?

Rof. Thus those will talk, who have not deceitful hearts.

> All my thoughts, all my love-affairs, all my fears, are, my dear father, well known to you.

SCENE II.

Pafcafio, then Timitilla.

Paf. What a manner of talking! very fine indeed! I am her father, and she shall obey me: what an impudent huzzy! So, so, Timitilla my dear ward is coming. Oh what a flame I feel in my heart at her fight! but I will withdraw, and watch her behaviour. [She goes on one fide.

Ti. Ladies and gentlemen behold Timitilla before you; I am an orphan, young, simple, and bashful; I am artless, and void of cunning; all that I desire is your favour, and I promise to have a grate-

ful sense of it. Unhappy me! I
now feel a fear entirely new,
which, good Heaven! I know
not how to express.

Paf. Excellent! This is very well, my *Timitilla*, by
being modest and reserved, you will always be esteem-
ed by every one.

Ti. Thank you, my guardian, I do what lies in my
power to gain esteem, (you don't know me yet.)

Paf. (Dear creature! she makes me more and more in
love with her.) Listen to me. *Rofmira* is to be married to Don *Sabbione* to-day.

Ti. 'It makes me mad.

Paf. Mad? why?

Ti. Because *Rofmira* hates him mortally, and frets
at it, and makes me fret too, at being left all alone.

Paf. She shall espouse him, depend upon it; but you
shan't be left alone——I love you better than my
daughter---Love prompts me---for those little pretty
eyes---do you understand?

Ti. Not I indeed.

Paf. Ah you little rogue, you take me.

Ti. What do my eyes do? Soon, speak.

Paf. When smiling, they give me life, when frowning,
death; wherefore, my dear, I desire you for my
spouse.

Ti. Don't squeeze me so hard, softly, softly, you hurt
me; (what a stupid creature!)

Paf. I suffer much worse myself.

Ti. 'Tis high time for me to go to the harpsicord.

Paf. Go then, but don't forget me.

Ti. O heaven! how you talk? adieu *Pafcafio*.

Paf. Adieu.

Ti. Don't be concerned, (if I was his wife, he would
not keep the cold from me) I will find the way to
get rid of him; and before I leave him, I will make
a fool of him a little.

Paf.

E promette d' esser grata.
Sventurata! adesso provo
Un timore affatto nuovo,
Che ridirlo, oh Dio! non sò.

Paf. Brava! così và ben, mia Timitilla;
Modesta, e ritirata'
Sarete da ciascun sempre stimata.
Ti. Grazie, signor Tutore;
Compisco il mio dover per farmi onore.
[Non mi conosci ancora.]
Paf. [Oh, cara! sempre più la m' innamora!]
Dammi mente. Rosmira in questo giorno
Don Sabbion sposerà. *Ti.* Sono arrabbiata.
Paf. Arrabiata? perchè? *Ti.* Perchè Rosmira
Odia a morte costui; perche tempesta,
É fammi tempestare,
Sola sola dovendomi lasciare.
Paf. Ella lo sposerà; non dubitate.
Voi sola non restate—
V' amo più che mia figlia—
L' amore mi consiglia—
Perchè quegli occhj belli—m' intendete?
Ti. Io per me nò. *Paf.* Furbetta, mi capite.
Ti. Che san questi occhj miei? presto, finite.
Paf. Pietosi mi dan vita, e fieri morte,
Onde, cara, vi bramo per consorte.
Ti. Non stringete; pian, pian; mi fate male.
[Oh, che sciocco animale!]
Paf. Io soffro peggio assai.
Ti. Al cembalo che io vada è tempo ormai.
Paf. Ite pur: ma di me non vi scordate.
Ti. Oh Ciel! come parlate? Addio, Pascasio.
Paf. Addio. *Ti.* Non vi rincresca.
[Se fossi moglie sua starei pur fresca!
Me ne vo' sbarazzare,
E nel partir lo voglio un po' burlare.]

Paf.

Paf. Vi fermate? *Ti.* Ora parto. Addio. *Paf.* Ad-
    dio.
Ti. [Oh fciocco!] *Paf.* Cofa c' è?
Ti. Non sò che fia
    Perdo ogni fenfo or che men vado via.

> *Care pupille belle,*
> *Voi fiete le mie stelle.*
> *Care pupille amate,*
> *La gioia mia, deh, fiate*
> *Il cor per voi nel petto*
> *Per gioia, per diletto*
> *Saltella, balzella,*
> *E ripofar non fa.*

SCENA III.

Pafcafio, indi Contrappunto, e Serpilla.

Paf. Ah, che dolci parole!
    'E un niente lo fciroppo di viole!
Con. Allegrezza, allegrezza! *Ser.* E viva, e viva.
Paf. Cofa è? *Con.* Lo fpofo arriva. *Paf.* Don
    Sabbione?
Ser. Appunto adeffo fale
    Sopra le voftre fcale. *Paf.* Addio, addio;
    Corro con effo a far l' obbligo mio. [*Parte.*
Con. Come dicevo.—*Ser.* Già per quefto incontro,
    Che avrà con Don Sabbione,
    Rofmira a mente fà la fua lezzione.
    Parliamo un pochettin del noftro amore.
Con. Sul voftro, e ful mio core
    Non c' è niente da dir; ma non ho un bezzo.
Ser. Eh, che l' oro non prezzo?
    La natura ci ha fatto tutti uguali:
    Bafta, che abbiamo i noftri capitali.

                              Con.

Paf. *Do you stay?*

Ti. *I am going now, adieu.*

Paf. *Adieu.*

Ti. [*Blockhead!*]

Paf. *What is the matter?*

Ti. *I don't know what is the matter? I lose my senses now that I am leaving you.*

> Dear pretty eyes, you are my luminaries; dear enchanting eyes, ye are my delight. For you with joy and pleasure, my heart within my breast leaps, bounds, and knows no rest.

S C E N E III.

Pascasio, afterwards Contrappunto and Serpilla.

Paf. *O what sweet words! Sweeter than honey.*

Con. *Joy, joy.*

Ser. *Let us sing and be merry.*

Paf. *What is the matter?*

Con. *The bridegroom is come.*

Paf. *What? Don Sabbione?*

Ser. *He is this very moment coming up stairs.*

Paf. *Good-bye, good-bye. I fly to pay my respects to him.* [*Exit.*

Con. *As I was saying.——*

Ser. *Rosmira has got her lesson by heart, against the meeting which she is to have with Don Sabbione. Let us talk a little about our love affairs.*

Con. *As to our hearts, there is nothing to say; but as to money, I have not a sous.*

Ser. *Oh, I don't mind money, nature has made us all equal, 'tis enough we have our persons.*

Con.

I

Con. *I don't deny it ; but we cannot feed upon love.
Love, believe me, soon grows cold.*

Ser. *Tell me are you, or are you not a master of mu-
ſic ?*

Con. *Certainly I am.*

Ser. *Very well, your profeſſion then is a profitable one.
And for my part, I am reſolved to go ſing upon the
ſtage : and thus money will roll in upon us.*

Con. *Perhaps ſo, perhaps not, for how difficult, alas !
will it be to meet with approbation ?*

Ser. *Pho, pho, much hazard indeed, one may do mira-
cles with the advantages of youth, gracefulneſs, and
beauty.*

Con. *Well, 'tis agreed. And for my part, in order
to render you miſtreſs of the art, I will make you
as much as poſſible, enter into the marrow of ſol, fa,
with the keys, naturals and flats: and provided you
add to all this a little aſſurance, every one will call
you a fine ſinger.*

*While the ſymphony is playing, the
haughty ſinger is treading the
ſtage, the air begins, and ſome
grand paſſage is to be executed
with gravity. A murmuring runs
thro' the audience ; they don't ſtay
for the cloſe, but they clap and
cry encore ; excellent, very well,
again, again ; 'till in compliance
with their noiſe, or to oblige
them, the haughty madam, begins again.*

SCENE

Con. Non nego; ma l' amore non ingrassa;
 L' amor, credete a me, che presto passa.

Ser. Dite, siete, o non siete
 Maestro di Cappella?

Con. Certo, lo sono. *Ser.* Oh, bella!
 Fate dunque un mestier, che dà profitto.
 Io nel pensier m' ho fitto
 Di far la Virtuosa;
 E i denari così verranno a iosa.

Con. Forse sì, forse nò. Che quanto, ahi, quanto
 Ci vuol poi per aver compatimento!

Ser. Puh, puh! che gran cimento!
 Miracoli si fa;
 Basta aver gioventù, grazia, & beltà.

Con. Ebben, siamo d' accordo. E per mia parte
 Per rendervi bravissima nell' arte,
 Penetrar vi farò
 Per quanto mai potrò
 La sol fa mi re do
 In sino alle midolle
 E le chiavi, e il bequadro, e il bemolle:
 E poi basta che siate un po' arrogante,
 E ciascun vi dirà brava cantante.

  Fin che suona il ritornello
  La fastosa Virtuosa
  Passeggiando se ne và.
  Viene l' aria, e un gran passaggio
  Eseguisce in gravità;
  Si bisbiglia nell' udienza,
  Non s' aspetta la cadenza,
  Ma si batte da chi ascolta,
  E si grida: un' altra volta,
  Viva, ben, da capo, ancora.
  Sia per chiasso, sia per spasso,
  La fastosa Virtuosa
  Torna l' aria a replicar.

   C   SCENA

SCENA IV.

Serpilla.

Eccomi ſul teatro a far da brava,
Or la parte di ſchiava, or di regina,
Or di ninfa, or di dama, or di pedina.
E perchè nò ? Sò fare un baciamano ;
Sò ſchizzare l' occhietto ;
Sò a tempo far l' inchino, ed il ghignetto ;
E sò con un ſol lazzo
Far venir l' acqua in bocca a più d' un pazzo,
In ſomma il perſonale, il garbo, il geſto,
Sarà tutto di ſeſto.   Al fin de' conti
Non mi confondo, nò : chè per avere
Di Virtuoſa il vanto,
Si sà, che a' noſtri dì non ci vuol tanto.

Ha un guſto da ſtordire
Chi canta in un Teatro !
Di là ſtà un Cicisbeo,
Che guarda, e che ſoſpira ;
Di quà ſi ſente dire,
Oh, come è ſpiritoſa !
Brava ! che bella coſa !
E dall' Udienza tutta
E viva replicar.

SCENE IV.

Serpilla alone.

Now behold me upon the stage, flaunting in the character of a slave, or of a queen, or of a country lass, or of a lady, or of one of the meaner sort. And why not? I know how to kiss my hands, I know how to ogle, I know how to make my compliments, and how to simper at a proper time: and with one single joke, to make more than one fool's mouth water. In short my person, my mien, my gesture, shall all be of a piece; In fine I shan't be out of countenance, no; for it is notorious, that now-a-days there is not so much required, to attain the name of a fine singer.

She that sings upon the stage, enjoys
an exquisite pleasure; on one side
stands a gallant, looking upon her
and sighing; on the other side, she
hears the sounds of " What a lively
girl! admirable, exceeding
fine," and all the audience resounds applause.

SCENE V.

An antichamber in Pascasio's house.

Don Sabbione with servants; afterwards Pascasio; then Timitilla, Serpilla, and Rosmira.

D. S.   Contented and gay the bridegroom
       appears; and transported with
       joy he goes singing, E la ra la
       le ra, e la ra la la.

*As the fashion is, I enter without ceremony, bride-
 groom-like, with freedom, and confidence.*

Pas. *My dear Don Sabbione, permit me to embrace
you, and clasp you to my bosom.*

D. S. *Most courteous Pascasio, father-in-law, father,
brother, uncle; see me here at length, come to do
you honour, and behold my hand ready to espouse you.*

Pas. *To espouse me? It is my daughter you are to
espouse.*

D. S. *Yes, your daughter is understood, and the whole
family. But why is she not here?*

Pas. *She shall be here immediately. Who is there?*

D. S. *Send the bride, for goodness sake.*

Pas. *Rosmira, here, Serpilla, Timitilla.*

D. S. *Mistress bride, your bridegroom is here, calling
and bawling for you.*

Pas. *Have patience, good Sir.*

D. S. *I am quite weary; ho, ho, let us make room,
here comes a drove of them.*

Pas. *D. Sabbione, I introduce you.*

D. S. *O my beautiful brides! more blooming than the
rose. I embrace you with the greatest fervency of
affection.*

            Pas.

SCENA V.

Anticamera in Casa di Pascasio.

*Don Sabbione con Servi, indi Pascasio, poi Timitilla,
Serpilla, e Rosmira.*

D. S.   Contento e brillante
            Già viene lo sposo,
            E tutto sfarzoso
            Cantando sen va,
            E la ra la le ra,
            E lo ra la la.

            Alla moda, alla moda,
            Entriam senza licenza,
            Da sposo, con franchezza, in confidenza.
Pas. Don Sabbione diletto,
            Lasciate che io v' abbracci, e stringa al petto.
D. S. Oh, Pascasio gentil, suocero mio,
            Padre, fratello, zio,
            Eccomi al fin venuto ad onorarvi,
            Ed ecco la mia man per isposarvi.
Pas. Per sposar me? Mia figlia sposerete.
D. S. Sì, la figlia, s' intende; e quanti siete.
            Ma perchè non è qui? Pas. Presto verrà.
            Oh, qualcun. D. S. La sposa io carità.
Pas. Rosmira, olà, Serpilla, Timitilla.
D. S. Sposa: lo sposo è qui, che chiama, e strilla.
Pas. Si dia pace, signor. D. S. Io son già stanco.
            Oh, oh, facciamo largo; eccone un branco.
Pas. Don Sabbion, vi presento——D. S. Oh, belle
            spose!
            Più fresche delle rose!
            Con amor straboccchevole v' abbraccio.
            4   Pas.

Paf. Eh, via, che fate mai? *D. S.* Che cofa faccio?
　　Tutte tre vo' fpofar. *Paf.* Quefta è la fpofa.
D. S. Lo so ch' è portentofa, ma lafciate,
　　Che io riconfronti ancora il fuo ritratto.
Ti. [Comincia bene!] *Ser.* [Oh, che volpone!]
　　　Paf. [E matto!]
D. S. Quegli occhj? nò. Quei labbri?
　　Quel volto? nò. Quel fronte?
　　Eh, il primo matrimonio vada a monte.
Paf. Perchè? qual fantafia vi falta in tefta?
D. S. Perchè quella mi piace più di quefta.
Paf. Cofpetto! *Rof.* Eh, padre! io non ci trovo
　　　male.
　　Serva. Spofi chi vuol, chè a me non cale.
　　　　　　　　　　　　　　　　[*Parte.*

Paf. Oh, rovinato me! Serpilla, vola
　　Prefto dietro a Rofmira, e la confola.
Ser. [Sì, sì: che furberia! Tutto ho comprefo.
　　E a chiappar Timitilla il laccio è tefo.]
　　　　　　　　　　　　　　　　[*Parte.*

D. S. Don Sabbione, fignora, a voi s' umilia.
Ti. Grazie, padrone mio,
　　La riverifco anche io.
D. S. Oh, che voce argentina!
　　Che beltà foprafina! Alò, Pafcafio,
　　Prefto prefto in un tratto
　　Facciam trà lei, trà me nuovo contratto.
Paf. Tale affronto! *Ti.* Signor, finiamo il giuoco,
　　Rifpondetemi un poco,
　　Chi v' ha detto fin ora
　　Che quella bella faccia m' innamora?
Paf. [Brava! feguite pur.] *Ti.* Forfe pigliate
　　La cafa di Pafcafio
　　Per il giardin d' amore,
　　Da fcegliere a piacere qualche fiore?
D. S. Sperai, Signora mia——*Ti.* Sperafte a torto.
　　[Fingo, non vacillate.]

　　　　　　　　　　　　　　　　　　Paf.

Paf. *Pshaw, what are you doing?*

D. S. *What am I doing? I would marry all three.*

Paf. *This is your bride.*

D. S. *I know it, and she is very handsome; but let me compare her picture with her.*

Ti. *(A good beginning.)*

Ser. *(What a fox.)*

Paf. *The fellow is a fool.*

D. S. *Those eyes? no, won't do. Those lips? that face? no. That forehead? Oh, I banish all thoughts of my first contract.*

Paf. *Why so? what crotchet have you got in your head now?*

D. S. *Because I like that lady better than this.*

Paf. *Very fine!*

Rof. *Dear father, I don't find it amiss. Your servant, marry whom you please, it is no concern of mine.* [Exit.

Paf. *Unhappy me! Serpilla, run immediately after Rosmira, and comfort her.*

Ser. *(Yes, yes, what a cheat; I understood it all, and the snare is ready to catch Timitilla.)* [Exit.

D. S. *Don Sabbione, Madam, offers his respects to you.*

Ti. *Thank you, Sir, I am your very humble servant.*

D. S. *O what melodious sounds! O what divine beauty! here, Pafcafio, quick, quick; let a new contract be drawn up betwixt her and me in an instant.*

Paf. *How provoking!*

Ti. *Sir, let the joke stop here. Answer me a word; who told you, that I am enamoured with that pretty face?*

Paf. *(Very well, follow it up.)*

Ti. *Perhaps you take Pafcafio's house for a garden of love, where you may pick and choose at pleasure.*

D. S. *I was in hopes, Madam.*

Ti. *You had no foundation for your hopes. (I am only feigning, don't waver.)*

Paf.

Paf. (O my dear life, you revive me. I am going away contented. You Timitilla, be faithful to me; and mark me, D. Sabbione, this is the conclusion, either marry my daughter, or get you gone from hence. I am master; I command, and will have it so.

You don't speak? what is the matter? Away, be gone, don't make my blood rise, Sir. If you won't have my daughter, there is no occasion for staying. Observe me well, I repeat it again, in two words, you may get you gone.

SCENE VI.

Timitilla and Don Sabbione.

Both. Ha, ha, ha, ha, ha, ha.

Ti. *Who can forbear laughing? ha, ha, an excellent beginning.*

D. S. *The ending will be better?*

Ti. *But Contrappunto and Serpilla have jointly entered into a league against me.*

D. S. *You must try to perplex them both, play tricks with them, and be resolute yourself.*

Ti. *I shall do then, as I have done hitherto, most heartily despise them.*

D. S. *Do you love me then, my dear?*

Ti. *I assure you of it.*

D. S. *Will you be mine seriously?*

Ti. *Yes, I swear I will.*

D. S.

Paſ. [Oh, cara anima mia! mi confolate!]
Contento me ne vò. Voi Timitilla,
Fate le parti mie. Voi, Don Sabbione,
Badate bene: ecco la conclufione.
O ſpofare mia figlia,
E partire di quì;
Son padrone, comando, e vo' così.

Lei non parla? che ſi fà?
'Eh, via, vada; non mi faccia,
Mio ſignore, riſcaldar.
Se mia figlia lei non vuole,
Non occorre quì reſtar.
Senta bene, in due parole
Lo ripeto un' altra volta
Lei ſen vada via di quì.

S C E N A   VI.

Timitilla, e Don Sabbione.

a 2. Ah, ah, ah, ah, ah, ah.
Ti. Chi può tener le rifa? oh, buon principio!
- *D. S.* Il fin farà miglior. *Ti.* Ma Contrappunto
    A Serpilla congiunto
    Fà contro di me lega. *D. S.* All uno e all'
    altra
    Voi datene una fredda, ed una calda;
    Burlatevi di loro; e ftate faldi.
Ti. Come ho fatto fin or dunque farò;
    Solennemente gli difprezzerò.
D. S. Dunque, cara, m' amate? *Ti.* Oh, v' affi-
    curo!
D. S. Sarete mia ful ferio? *Ti.* Oh, ve lo giuro!
D D. S.

D. S. Quei dolci, e cari occhietti
   Saranno tutti miei? *Ti.* Sì.   *D. S.* Quel boc-
      chino
   Sarà tutto per me? *Ti.* Sì.   *D. S.* Quel visino
   'E tutto tutto mio? *Ti.* Sì, tutto tutto.
D. S. Anche io voltro farò tutto, e poi tutto.

> *Quel bell' occhietto,*
> *Quel bell' visetto,*
> *Mi fà languir :*
> *E sento già*
> *Nel petto mio*
> *Un grande ardore,*
> *Che accende il core*
> *Or quà or là.*
> *Odi il fracaffo,*
> *Odi il rumore,*
> *Che nel mio core*
> *Si sente già.*

SCENA VII.

Timitilla.

Oh, che gran differenza
C' è trà Paccafio e Don Sabbione! E pure
La politica vuol, che io fcarti il vecchio
Con finezza, e bel bello,
E a poco a poco che io gli dia martello.
Per altro la mia fcelta è vella e fatta ;
La natura l' ifpira, e non fon matta.

> *Ah, fon pur troppo rari !*
> *Ah, vedo, e non m' inganno !*
> *Quegli occhj cari cari*
> *Mi fanno delirar.*

SCENE

D. S. *Shall thofe dear bewitching eyes be all mine ?*

Ti. *Yes.*

D. S. *Shall that little mouth be all for me.*

Ti. *Yes.*

D. S. *And that pretty face all mine ?*

Ti. *Yes, all, all.*

D. S. *I too will be yours, and yours entirely.*

> That pretty little eye, that pretty little
> face, make me languifh with defire ;
> and already I feel within my bofom,
> a vehement flame, which fets my heart
> on fire on every fide. Hark, hear the
> cracking, hear the noife which is now
> making in my heart.

SCENE VII.

Timitilla alone.

How great is the difference betwixt Pafcafio and D.
Sabbione ! and yet prudence requires me to dif-
card the old man artfully and cautioufly, and to
break with him by degrees. However, my choice
is compleatly made, nature fuggefts it, and I am
no fool.

> O how admirable are they. O ! I fee
> it, and am not deceived ; thofe
> dear, dear eyes fet me befide my-
> felf.

S C E N E VIII.

A garden in Pafcafio's houfe.

Serpilla, Contrappunto, and Lindoro.

Ser. *Don't make me fay it over and ever again ; yes,*
D. Scbbione faid, what I have told you.

Con. *I promife you then, that upon this difcovery, I*
found my revenge.

Ser. *May I be certain of it ?*

Con. *Its certain as that I love you.*

Ser. *My dear, you give me great comfort, I defire no*
more.

Lin. *You will do well: for fhe gives herfelf fo many*
airs, that it is but right to humble her pride.

Ser. *Very true : fhe prides herfelf in every thing, and*
fets herfelf formoft in every thing ; fhe is a trouble-
fome, and truly tirefome creature.

Lin. *See, here fhe is coming directly.*

Con. *And fhe fhall find fome forrow : now, for an*
artful ftroke, Serpilla. Let us go one fide, and I
will tell you what we muft do in concert.

Ser. *Very well, you are a brave man. Let us now*
ftrike together while the iron is hot.

[Contrappunto and Serpilla go on one fide.

Con. *You muft go away too.*

Lin. *This is my method when the weather is bad, I*
take myfelf out of it, and without making any di-
fturbance, I go where my heart is always fighing to
be. I go with joy to find Rofmira.

> If I could but at this moment exprefs my
> pleafure and fatisfaction, I fhould in-
> fpire every breaft with perfect ferenity.

SCENE

SCENA VIII.

Giardino in casa di Pascasio.

Serpilla Contrappunto, e Lindoro.

Ser. Non mel fate ridir. Sì. Don Sabbione
Parlò come v' ho detto.
Con. Adunque io vi prometto,
Che con questa scoperta
La vendetta farò. *Ser.* Posso star certa?
Con. Quanto è certo che v' amo.
Ser. Caro, mi consolate: altro non bramo.
Lin. Farete bene. Ha tanti grilli in testa,
Ch' è giusto d' abbassarle un po' la cresta.
Ser. È verissimo: in tutto ella si stima;
In tutto ella pretende esser la prima.
È una noia, una vera seccatura.
Lin. Eccola quà che viene a dirittura.
Con. E troverà de' guai. Serpilla, all' arte:
Tiriamoci in disparte; e di concerto
Dirò che s' hà da far. *Ser.* Bene: vi lodo;
Battiamo uniti ora ch' è caldo il chiodo.
[Contrappunto e Serpilla vanno in disparte.
Con. Partite ancora voi. *Lin.* Questo è il mio
patto;
Quando fà brutto tempo io me la batto.
E senza far rumore
Vado dove il mio core ognor sospira;
Vado contento a ritrovar Rosmira.

Se il piacer, se il mio contento,
Se dicessi in tal momento;
Io farei goder a ogni alma
Calma placida nel cor.

SCENA

SCENA IX.

Serpilla e Contrappunto, indi Timililla, poi Don Sab-
bione, e dopo Pafcafio.

Ser. In verità voi fiete un gran cervello!
Con. Vo' che vada a pennello. E il fondamento,
Ricordatevi ben, voglio che fia
Un motivo real di gelofia.
Ser. Sì, sì; gl' innamorati
Si crederanno tutti due burlati.
Oh, con quanto gran gufto
L' orgogliofa vedrei
Da tutti i cicifbei piantata là!
Con. Quefto fuccederà. Bafta, che uniti
Di Don Sabbione, e di Pafcafio in faccia
Gridiamo, efageriamo,
E contro lei con forza ftrepitiamo.
Ser. Lafciate fare a me. Già per natura
Ho la lingua un po' lunga. Non temete.
Spirito non mi manca; fentirete.
Farò veder chi fono.
Con. Eccola. Zitti. A noi. **Ser.** Viene ora il
buono.

> [*Vanno un pochino in difparte.*

Ti. *Ombre amene, in voi fol trovo*
La mia pace, e la mia quiete
Sì, voi fole poffedete
Il fegreto del mio cor.
Ser. } *Che fi fà per di quà?*
Con. } *Signorina, dove và?*
Ti. *Qual piacerè, oh Dio! trovate*
Nel turbare il mio ripofo?
Ah, rifpondervi non ofo!
L'andar via farà miglior.

Ser.

SCENE IX.

Serpilla and Contrappunto, then Timitilla, afterwards Don Sabbione, and laſt of all Paſcaſio.

Ser. In truth you have a good head-piece of your own.

Con. I warrant you we ſhall meet with no rubs, and for the foundation of the whole (mark me well) I deſign that there ſhall be a real object of jealouſy.

Ser. Yes, yes, the loving couple will find themſelves both fooled; O! with how great pleaſure ſhould I ſee the proud Madam forſaken by all her gallants.

Con. That will be the conſequence. It is ſufficient that we cry, exaggerate, and exclaim ſtrenuouſly againſt her before Don Sabbione and Paſcaſio.

Ser. Leave that to me, I was born with a long tongue, ſo don't be afraid. You ſhall find I don't want ſpirit, I will ſhow what I am.

Con. Here ſhe is! Huſh! Now to our parts.

Ser. Now comes the cream of the jeſt.

                [They go a little on one ſide.

Ti.   O ye pleaſant ſhades, in you alone I find
                peace and quiet, yes, you alone poſ-
                ſeſs the ſecret of my heart.

Ser. }   What are you doing this way ?
Con. }   Madam, where are you going ?

Ti.   Good God what pleaſure do you find in
                diſturbing my repoſe ? I dare not
                anſwer you, it will be better to leave
                you.

Ser.   } If you are for going, Madam,
Con. } Take yourself a thousand miles off.

D. S.   Where are you going, my Timitilla?
           Where are you going my dear love?

Ser.   } O Sir it is well known
Con. } She is going away with Pascasio,

Ti.   Ye abusive creatures, you affront me in-
           sufferably.

Ser.   } Forgive me, pardon me,
Con. } For my boldness.

D. S.   Come along with me, don't mind them
           you shall be my dear bride.

Ti.   Sabbione shall be the protector of a poor
           orphan.

Ser.   } No, Sabbione shall be the protector
Con. } Of Pascasio's dear.
           And you poor blockhead
           Shall feel the smart.

D. S.   How? Pascasio's dear?

Ser.   } So it is,
Con. } Her heart is not for you.

D. S.   Get you gone, if you are another's.

Ti.   Alas! All the deceitful world is combined
           against me.

Pas.   What is the matter Timitilla? My de-
           light, my dear ward! what is the
           matter my jewel?

Ser.   } She is with Sabbione,
Con. } Who is the happy man
           That enjoys her heart.

Pas.   With Sabbione?

Ser.   } Yes Sir.
Con. }

Pas.   Stay then there, an ungrateful creature!
           I will no longer have pity for you.

Ti.

Ser. }	*Vada pur, se se ne và,*
Con. }	*Mille miglia via di quà.*
D. S.	*Dove vai, mia Timitilla?*
	Dove vai, mio dolce amor?
Ser. }	*Sì, signore, già si sà ;*
Con. }	*Con Pascasio se ne và.*
Ti.	*Maldicenti! m' insultate,*
	Non avete carità.
'Ser. }	*Mi condoni, mi perdoni*
Con. }	*Della mia temerità.*
D. S.	*Vien con me ; non ci badare ;*
	Tu sarai la mia sposina.
Ti.	*D' una povera pupilla*
	Sia Sabbione il difensor.
Ser. }	*Sia Sabbione il protettor .*
Con. }	*Dell' amata di Pascasio ;*
	E voi, povero minchione
	Resterete col brucior.
D. S.	*Di Pascasio ?* Ser. } *Così è.* Con. }
	E il suo cor non è per te.
D. S.	*Vanne pur, se d' altri sei.*
Ti.	*Ah, congiura a' danni miei*
	Tutto il mondo traditor !
Pas.	*Che cosa hai, mia Timitilla ?*
	Ah, mio ben ! Ah, mia pupilla !
	Che cosa hai, mio bel tesor ?
Ser. }	*Con Sabbione se ne stà,*
Con. }	*Ch' è l' amato fortunato,*
	Che il suo cor si goderà.
Pas.	*Con Sabbione ?* Ser. } *Sì, signore.* Con. }
Pas.	*Resta pure, ingrato core,*
	Più di te non ho pietà.

E   Ti.

Ti.   . *Sventurata ! Sciagurata !*
        Ah, di me cosa farà?

Paſ.   *Resta pur con Don Sabbione.*

D. S.   *Vanne pure con Pascasio.*

Ser. }
Con. } *Bella, bella in verità.*

Ti.   *Ah, Tutor ! Paſ. Più non t' ascolto.*

Ti..   *Ah, Signor ! D. S. Non son sì stolta.*

Ti.   *Ah, ch' enorme falsità !*

Ser. }
Con. } *Mi perdoni, mi condoni,*
        Della mia temerità.

Ti.   *Ma sentite in carità !*

a. 4.   *Nò, per te non v' è pietà.*
        Chi d', un sol non si contenta,
        Si martelli, se ne penta,
        A chi finge così và.
        Nò, per te non v' è pietà.

Ti.   *Ma sentite in carità !*

Fine dell' Atto Primo.

Ti.   Miferable and wretched that I am! Alas
         what will become of me.
Paf.   Stay, ftay, with Don Sabbione.
D. S. Go, go, along with Pafcafio.
Ser. }
Con. } Admirable, admirable, indeed!

Ti.   Alas, my guardian!
Paf.   I will hear no more.
Ti.   Alas, dear Sir!
D. S. I am not fuch a fool.
Ti.   Alas, what an enormous falfehood!
Ser. } Forgive me, pardon me.
Con. } For my boldnefs.
Ti.   Do but hear me for goodnefs fake.
All four. No, for you there is no pity; thofe that
         are not contented with one only,
         will be plagued and foon have reafon
         to repent, and fo it will happen to
         thofe that diffemble; for you there
         is no pity.
Ti.   Do but hear me, for goodnefs-fake.

End of the Firft Act.

ACT II.

SCENE I.

An Anti-chamber adjoining to Pascasio's Garden.

Lindoro with a Bundle of Roses, Contrappunto of Jeffamins, Don Sabbione with Tulips, Rosmira with Violets, Timitilla with Junquils, and Serpilla with an Amaranthus, one after another.

Lin. 'THESE blushing roses, which I have gathered for my love, are all without prickles, so the affection which I carry in my bosom, is without bitterness.

Con. This beautiful jeffamin, which I bear as a present to my love, refembles my heart in whiteness, simplicity, and softness.

D. S. This dear tulip, I design as a present for my fair, one day or other she will perhaps, give me something else in return.

All three. How beautiful are the flowers, how sweet is love! How dear is happiness.

Ros. These charming violets, which I myself have plucked, are all designed for my dear Lindoro, the worthy object of my love.

Ti.

ATTO II.

SCENA I.

Anticamera contigua al Giardino di Pascafio.

Lindoro con un mazzo di Rose, Contrappunto di Gelso-
mini, Don Sabbione di Tulipani, Rosmira di Viole,
Timittilla di Gioncbiglie, e Serpilla con un Amaranto,
l' uno succcssi, vanente dopo l' altro.

Lin.   QUESTE rose porporine,
            Che ho raccolto pel mio bene,
            Sono tutte senza spine,
          Come senza amare pene,
          E l' effetto che ho nel sen.

Con.   Questo vago gelsomino,
          Che al mio bene io reco in dono,
          Candidetto come io sono,
          Semplicetto, tenerino,
          S' assomiglia al mio bel cor.

D. S. Questo caro tulipano
          Vo' donarlo alla mia bella ;
          Qualche cosa ancora ella
          Forse un dì mi donerà.

a. 3. Vaghi fiori, dolci amori,
          Cara mia felicità !

Ros.   Queste belle violette
          Da me stessa raddunate,
          Sono tutte destinate
          A Lindoro, mio tesoro,
          Degno oggetto del mio amor.

                              Ti.

Ti.   *Questa tenera gionchiglia*
E' odorosa a maraviglia,
E vo' farne un regaletto,
Che fia prova al mio diletto
Della mia sincerità.

Sa.   *Questo amabile Amaranto*
Io presento a Contrappunto :
Verde è sempre come appunto
La mia bella fedeltà.

a. 6.   *Vaghi fiori, dolci amori*
Cara mia felicità !

Con. Oh, bravi tutti quanti!
Ser. Mettiam da banda i canti. Io con colei
   Per un tesoro qui non resterei.
Lin. Pascasio è nelle furie. *D. S.* Ebben? Ci resti ;
   E' tutto uno per me, se goda, o pesti.
   Basta, che Timitilla tenga duro.
Ti. State pure di me più che sicuro.
Ser. Sì, eh, signora mia? *Ti.* Sì, sì, da vero ;
   E le cabale vostre io stimo un zero.   [*Parte.*
D.S. Dunque ogn' un pensi a se. Schiavo, padroni.
                         [*Parte.*

Ser. Ora sì, che non sento più ragioni.
   Vo' far contro di lor quel che potrò ;
   Certo la spunterò.
   Andiamo Contrappunto. *Con.* Andiam, ma
     spesso
   Per fare in fretta, e non aver giudizio,
   Vanno i più belli intrighi in precipizio.
                    [*Partono insieme.*
Ros. Parto, mio bene, anche io. Veggio venire
   Pascasio, e Don Sabbion. Per ottenere
   Il vostro cor che unicamente adoro,
   Sò quel che devo fare: addio Lindoro. [*Parte.*
Lin. Quella dolce certezza,
   Ch' è di sua tenerezza unico pegno,
   E' l' amabil sostegno di mia vita ;
   Perchè ogni pena mia veggo finita.

                              Grato

Ti. This delicate junquil is wonderfully sweet, and I intend to make a little present of it, that it may be to my beloved a proof of my sincerity.

Ser. This smiling amaranthus I present to Contrappunto, it is fair and flourishing, as my unshaken constancy.

All Six. How beautiful are the flowers! How sweet is love! How dear is happiness!

Con. *Well done all of us!*

Ser. *Let us leave off singing, I would not stay here with her for the world.*

Lin. *Pascasio is in a rage.*

D. S. *Well, so let him be. 'Tis all the same to me, whether he be merry or sad. I shall be contented, if Tintillla but stands her ground.*

Ti. *Rest satisfied with regard to me.*

Ser. *Is it so, my lady?*

Ti. *Yes, yes, indeed, and I set your caball at nought.* [Exit.

D. S. *Let every one then think for himself. Your servant gentle folks.* [Exit.

Ser. *Now I will no longer listen to reason. I will do every thing against them, that lies in my power, and shall certainly gain my ends; let's go Contrappunto.*

Con. *We'll go, but let's remember, that doing things in a hurry without consideration, often ruins the best-laid schemes.* —— [They go out together.

Ros. *I am going to my dear. I see Pascasio and Don Sabbione coming, I know what I must do to obtain your heart, which alone is the object of my adoration. Adieu, Lindoro.* [Exit.

Lin. *This agreeable assurance, which is a singular proof of her affection, makes my life happy, as I now see all my cares at an end.*

Pro-

ACT II.

Propitious Love, do not diſturb the
dear repoſe of my boſom, and oh!
make me not feel the pains of cruel
ſuſpicion.

SCENE II.

Paſcaſio and D. Sabbione quarrelling; afterwards
Timitilla.

Paſ. This is very impertinent of you.

D. S. I loſe all patience.

Paſ. Faith! 'tis very fine. Would you compare your-
ſelf to me?

D. S. Would you ſtand in competition with D. Sabbione?

Paſ. What are your merits?

D. S. I am handſomer, and younger than you.

Paſ. I am in the prime of life.

D. S. In the prime of life? ha, ha.

Paſ. You! you have no concern with her.

D. S. You may lick your lips at her.

Paſ. She promiſed me her affection.

D. S. To me ſhe ſwore fidelity.

Paſ. You lie.

D. S. You are an old dotard.

Paſ. And you a coward.

D. S. Do you call me coward? I defy you to a mortal
combat.

Paſ. I'll go in for my ſword, and hew you in pieces in
an inſtant.

As they are going out in a rage they meet
Timitilla.

Ti.

Grato amor, la cara pace
Non turbar in questo petto;
Nè con barbaro sospetto,
Deh, non farmi palpitar.

SCENA II.

Pascasio e Don Sabbione altercando; poi Timitilla.

Pas. Questa è un' impertinenza!
D. S. Mi scappa la pazienza!
Pas. Oh questa è bella affè!
  Ti vuoi metter con me? *D. S.* Con Don Sab-
    bione
  Vuoi stare a paragone?
Pas. Quai sono i pregj tuoi?
D. S. Son più bello, e più giovine di voi;
Pas. Io son di fresca età.
D. S. Di fresca età! ah, ah.
Pas. A voi? non ve ne tocca.
D. S. Nettatevi la bocca.
Pas. A me promise affetto.
D. S. A me fede giurò. *Pas.* Siete bugiardo.
D. S. Voi siete rimbambito. *Pas.* E voi co-
  dardo.
D. S. Codardo a me? Ti sfido in gran duello.
Pas. Vò a prendere la spada, e ti sbudello.
     [*Nel partire furiosi incontrano Timitilla.*

Ti. Piano, fignori miei, non tanto foco ;
    In dietro, adagio, adagio un poco.
    Il foggetto qual' è di quefta lite?

Paf. Venite quà. *D. S.* Sentite.

Paf. Finiamo quefta trefca.
    Timitilla, di fceglier non v' increfca
    Un di noi per marito
    Quello che vol ftimate il più gradito.

D. S. Son contento. [Lo fcelto io fon di certo.]

Paf. [Già mi poffo fidar del proprio merto.]

Ti. [Ci vuole arte!] *D. S.* Gradite la mia fede?

Ti. In quefto feno il voftro cor rifiede.

Paf. Sarete mia? *Ti.* dimani. [Oh, la fbagliate!]

D. S. Chi volete? *Paf.* Parlate. *D. S.* E lui?
      Paf. Sono io?

Ti. Voi fiete——fiete voi—Signori, addio.

Paf. Mi lafciate così? *D. S.* Quefto è l' amore?

Ti. Altre volte fpiegai tutto il mio core.
    [Pafcafio, voi fapete il ben che adoro.]
    [Don Sabbion, fol per voi languifco e moro.]

          Di quefto fen l' ardore,
          Caro, tu folo fei ;
          Luce degli occhj miei,
          Io fida a te farò.

D. S.   Che miro fventurato!
          Delufo io fon reftato!
          Non poffo più parlar.

Paf.   Obimè! cofa ho veduto?
          Mi veggia già perduto!
          Non sò che debbo far.

Ti. *Softly, gentlemen, not fo furious; back again, back again; be a little cool. What is the caufe of your quarrel?*

Paf. *Come this way?*

D. S. *Mind.*

Paf. *Let us put an end to this difpute, Timitilla, don't refufe to choofe one of us for your hufband, whom you efteem the moft agreeable.*

D. S. *I agree to it.* (*I am certain of the preference.*)

Paf. (*Now, I may truft to my own merit.*)

Ti. (*Now for a piece of art.*)

D. S. *Will you accept my hand?*

Ti. *In this bofom your heart is placed.*

Paf. *Will you be mine?*

Ti. *To-morrow.* (*Oh you are miftaken.*)

D. S. *Which will you have?*

Paf. *Speak.*

D. S. *Is it he?*

Paf. *Am I the happy man?*

Ti. *You are——you are——Gentlemen, your fervant.*

Paf. *Do you leave me fo?*

D. S. *Is this your love?*

Ti. *I have opened my whole heart before now.* (*You know Pafcafio, the man whom I adore*) (*It is for you alone D. Sabbione, that I languifh and die.*)

> You my dear have infpired my breaft
> with a mutual flame.   [*To D. Sab.*
> O delight of my eyes, I will be ever
> faithful to you.   [*To Paf.*

D. S.   What do I fee, wretched that I am, I
am deceived, I am ftruck dumb.

Paf.   Alas! what have I feen? I find myfelf
undone, I don't know what to do.

Ti.   Unhappy me! I have miffed my aim, I find myfelf entangled, I can fcarcely breathe.

D. S.   Shall I kill him? no, I will be gone.

Paf.   Shall I ftay or go?

Ti.   What then will become of me.

D. S.   What am I to think?

Paf.   What am I to refolve upon?

Ti.   O my heart, what do you fuggeft?

All three. O what plague is this! For ever accurfed be love.

SCENE III.

A hall in Pafcafio's houfe, with a harpficord and chairs.

Contrappunto and Serpilla; afterwards Timitilla.

Ser. O *what a noife! what confufion! did you hear it?*

Con. Yes; *but let us pretend not to know any thing of the matter, left we hurt our own affairs; and Timitilla, by defiring to fhow too much fpirit, fhall bring herfelf into a frefh fcrape.*

Ser. Let her; *I fhall be glad to fee it. We will ftick clofe to her fkirts.*

Con. Yes, *but have a little patience.——*

Ser. But *if fhe affronts me? I give it up; I would not then be patient for a million of money.*

Con. Now *is the time to receive your inftructions; here Serpilla quick. Timitilla will be here prefently; let us fing fome little thing in the interim; come to the harpficord.*

                        Ser.

TI.	*Mefchina! I' ho fbagliata!*
	Mi vedo già imbrogliata!
	Non poffo refpirar.
D. S.	*L' uccido? nò; mi parto.*
Paf.	*M' arrefto, o vado via?*
Ti.	*Dunque di me che fia?*
D. S.	*Che penfo? Paf. che rifolvo?*
Ti.	*Che mi configli, o cor?*
a 3.	*Oh, che difgrazia è quefta!*
	Sia maledetto amor!

S C E N A III.

Sala in cafa di Pafcafio con Cembalo, e fedie.

Contrappunto, e Serpilla, indi Timitilla.

Ser. Oh che rumor! oh, che fracaffo! Udifte?
Con. Sì; ma facciam le vifte
    Di non faperne niente. -Intorbidare
    Potremmo il noftro affare. E Timitilla
    Col voler far da brava un poco troppo,
    Inciamperà di nuovo in qualche intoppo.
Ser. Inciampi pur: ci averò gufto: addoffo
    Noi fteffi le daremo a più non poffo.
Con. Sì; ma un pochin di fiemma——**Ser.** E fe
    m' infulta?
    Chi s' è vifto, s' è vifto:
    Per un miglion di fcudi io non refifto.
Con. Di prender la lezzione il tempo è quefto.
    Alò, Serpilla, prefto. Timitilla
    Starà poco a venir. Qualche cofetta
    Cantiamo in quefto mentre; alla fpinetta.

Ser. Non mi faccio pregare. Ecco una scelta
    Di canzoni rarissime,
    Patetiche, andantine, ed allegrissime.
Con. Quale vi piace più? *Ser.* Per me è lo stesso.
Con. Cominciam dalla prima. Attenta adesso. I
    Cappari! tre bemolli! *Ser.* Io già v'ho detto,
    E vi ridico ancora in fede mia,
    Che il bemolle non sò che cosa sia.

        Grazie agl' inganni tuoi,
        Al fin respiro, o Nice.——

Con. Nò, questa è troppo vecchia: alla seconda.

Ser.   *Un certo non sò che,*
        Non sò se m' inten——

Con. Peggio, peggio, Serpilla. Ella è vecchis-
    sima,
Ser. La terza è eccellentissima,
    Sopra d' uno smorfioso,
    Composta in Venezian stile grazioso.

       L' amor mio, Ninetta cara,
       Xe arrivà fora del segno,
       Che a soffrirlo è troppo impegno,
       E l' è un' atto di virtù.

       Mi me par che tutto el fogo
       Dell' inferno abbia nel petto,
       E del mal mio maledetto,
      Caro ben, sè causa vu.

Con. Brava Serpilla cara!
Ti. Brava, da capo, ancora: oh, cosa rara!
    Il signor Contrappunto

                    Chiaro

Ser. I won't give you the trouble to press me. Here is a collection of very choice airs; some slow, some quicker, some very quick.

Con. Which pleases you best?

Ser. 'Tis the same to me.

Con. Let us begin with the first: now mind. Bless me! three flats!

Ser. I have already told you, and now I tell you again, upon my word, I don't know what a flat is.

> Thanks to your coquetting tricks; at
> length I am free, o Nice.—

Con. Pshaw! that is too old; on, to the second.

Ser.   A certain thing I know not what; pray,
        do you under—

Con. Worse and worse; this is as old as my grand-mother.

Ser. The third is very fine; made upon a coxcomb, and composed in an elegant Venetian stile.

> My love, dearest Kitty, exceeds all bounds,
>   that it is too much for me to bear, and
>   becomes an act of virtue.

> Methinks all the fire in hell has seized
>   my bosom, and you, my life, are
>   the cause of this accursed misfor-
>   tune.

Con. Well done, my dear Serpilla.

Ti. Well done, again encore, excellent! It is plain to be seen, that Mr. Contrappunto takes all the care of

the

the charming Serpilla, and none at all of Timitilla.
Well, patience, patience.

Ser. [*She begins with her accustomed rudeness.*]
Con. *I discharge my duty equally to both of you.*
Ti. *Oh, 'tis very evident. I wish you joy, Madam.*
Ser. *I congratulate you in my turn.*
Ti. *Very fine, Madam?*
Ser. *Your ladyship enchants every body.*
Ti. *Your ladyship makes every body in love with you.*
Ser. *silly girl.*
Ti. *Foolish wench.*
Con. *Fie! hold your tongues! will you expose your-*
selves?
Ser. *She begun first.*
Ti. *Fine again. Truth is a good thing; but you op-*
pose my union with D. Sabbione.
Ser. *I am glad you know it.*
Ti. *What? again?*
Ser. *From the little you have seen, you may judge what*
is to come.
Con. *Hold, hold a little for heaven's sake, let us go*
on with our lesson. 'Tis your turn, Timitilla, come
this way, and sing.
Ser. [*Now there will be a fine discord.*]

Ti.   Think how to fix my charmer—
Con.   Think how to fix my charmer—
Ti.   Think how to fix my charmer.—

Ser. [*She cannot sing a single note; how it pleases*
me!]
Con. *If I know any thing of my art, here are three*
sharps.
Ti. *What is it to me if there were six?*
Con. *Grant me patience. Let us begin again, come.*
Ser. [*The poor ignorant creature does not know where*
she is.]

                                              Ti.

Chiaro fi vede che ha tutto l' impegno
Per la bella Serpilla,
Niente per Timitilla; e ben pazienza.
Ser. [Comminciam colla folita infolenza.]
Con. Fò il mio dovere con ugual premura.
Ti. Oh, il fatto l' afficura! Io bramerei
Rallegrarmi con lei. *Ser.* Vo' farè anche io
Con lei l' obbligo mio. *Ti.* Brava, Signora!
Ser. Ella ciafcuno incanta! *Ti.* Ella innamora!
Ser. Frafchetta! *Ti.* Pazzarella! *Con.* Olà, tacete:
Far nafar vi volete? *Ser.* Effa è la prima.
Ti. Oh, brava ancor! La verità fi ftima!
Voi però con Sabbion mi traverfate.—
Ser. Ho piacer lo fappiate. *Ti.* Ancor di più?
Ser. Se poco è quel che lù,
Potete preveder quel che farà.
Con. Zitte, zitte, un pochin per carità.
Seguitiam la lezzione.
Tocca a voi, Timitilla,
Venite quà, cantate.
Ser. [Ora fi fentiran delle ftuonate!]

Ti.   *Penfa a ferbarmi, o care—*
Con.   *Penfa a ferbarmi, o caro—*
Ti.   *Penfa a ferbarmi, o caro.—*

Ser. [Non ne dice una nota. Oh, che piacere!]
Con. Se è vero il mio meftiere,
Tre diefis fon quefti agli occhj miei.
Ti. Che importa a me, fe follero anche fei?
Con. Che pazienza! Torniam da capo, via.
Ser. [Non sà l' ignorantella ove fi fia.]

Ti. *Penfa a ferbarmi, o caro,*
    I dolci affetti tuoi—— ..

Con. Oibò! Quefto è un gran fallo.
    Quefto è un fropofitaccio da cavallo.

Ti. Cofa dire volete?

Con. Che voi ftuonate maledettamente.

Ti. Andate via ; non ne fapete niente.
    Io ne sò più di voi. Che? voi ridete?
    Ora mi fentirete ; ;
    ·Quì, quì, ful voftro vifo
    Voglio un' aria cantare all' improvifo.
    Io fon quella che fono : e ogni un mi loda.

Ser. [Virtuofa da vero a tutta moda.]

Ti.   *Vedo ben, che voi volete*
        Un po' troppo alzar la tefta ;
        Ma fignore mio garbato, [a Contrappunto.
        Bel vifino delicato,   [a Serpilla.
        La mi fcufi, la m' intenda,
        Favorifca, non fi offenda ;
        Cari, cari, foggettini,
        Proverete, fentirete,
        Quel che penfo, e che sò far.
        Come due pulcin bagnati,
        Zitti, zitti, fpennacchiati,
        Refterete chini, chini
        Il mio garbo ad ammirar.

Ser. Ben? colla voftra flemma? avete udito?
Con. Ah, me la lego al dito! Ser. Ah! quefta volta
    Non vo' che l' ira mia refti fepolta!
Con. Sepolta non ftarà. Cara Serpilla,
    Già la mia mente ftilla
    * Di vendicarci il modo. Ser. E quando? Con.
    Adeffo.
Ser. Gli affronti, che ci fà, vanno all' eccetto.

                               Con.

Ti.   Think how to fix, my charmer thy
          dearest dearest love.

Con. Fie, fie, this is very bad, it is a shameful error.
Ti. What do you mean?
Con. That you make a confounded discord.
Ti. Get you gone, you know nothing of the matter. I
     know more than you. What? do you laugh? You
     shall hear me immediately, upon the spot, sing an air
     extempore. I know what I am myself, and I have
     the esteem of every one.
Ser. She is a true fashionable singing girl.

Ti.   I very well perceive that you have a mind to
          hold up your heads a little too high, but my
          very good Sir, [to Contrappunto.] my mild els
          pretty face, [to Serpilla.] Be so kind as to listen
          to me, and pray don't be offended, my dear
          Sir, my dear madam, you shall find to your cost,
          what I design to do. Like two little chickens
          bemired and stript of their feathers, you shall be
          silenced and humbled, envying my prosperity.

Ser. Well, Mr. Patience, did you hear her?
Con. Oh, I'll set it down in my book.
Ser. I will not now keep my anger within bounds.
Con. There is no occasion. My dear Serpilla, I am
     now hatching the means of revenge.
Ser. But when?
Con. Immediately.
Ser. The affronts which we receive are intolerable.

Con. See the old man is coming : get away.

Ser. N*, I'll help you, rail againſt her.

Con. 'Tis not proper now. Get you gone; but farther, I beg you, if you happen to meet *Timtilla*, that you would diſſemble your anger.

Ser. Nay, if I fall into her company, and muſt not let a word drop againſt her, it will certainly choak me.

Con. Conſider, I am affronted as well as you, follow my advice. Do you underſtand me ? you have a ſpirit fit for any thing ; have your wits about you.

Ser. The more I think of it, the more I am enraged ; I don't know what this fooliſh girl means, ſhe will not only have her drove of lovers ; but what is worſe, even under my noſe will ſhe be playing, dancing, and ſinging with a thouſand gallants, and ſpitefully pluming herſelf and flaunting. Oh but if I am put in a paſſion, you ſhall ſee ſome fine ſport, when we are oppoſed to each other, it will ſoon be known which of us is the more able,

> I am good natured to a certain pitch ; but if I am provoked, I'll make that impudent huſſey tremble. Will ſhe put herſelf in competition with me ? Ha, ha, it makes me laugh. Poor ſimpleton ! No, ſhe has not ſo much merit. If ſhe ſhould provoke me again, I ſhall know how to revenge myſelf, I ſhall

Con. Ecco il vecchio che vien : partite.. **Ser.** Nò:
A dir mal di colei v' aiuterò.

Con. Or non è tempo : andate : anzi vi prego,
Se Timitilla mai voi rincontrate,
L' ira diffimulate. **Ser.** Oh ! fe la trovo,
E fcappar non mi deve una parola,
Son certa, mi verrà tanto di gola.

Con. Penfate, che ancor io fono l' offefo :
Seguite il mio configlio. Avete intefo ?
Voi fiete un fpiritello,
Che di tutto sà far. State in cervello.

Ser. Più ch ci penfo, più mi vien la rabbia.
Non sò che cofa s' abbia quefta frafca
Non fol gli amanti vuole uno per tafca ;
Ma quel ch' è peggio ancor ; fugli occhj miei
Con mille cicifbei,
Se fuona, balla, o canta,
Si pavoneggia alle mie fpalle, e vanta.
Ah ! fe mi falta al fin la mofca al nafo,
Vo' fi veda un bel cafo. A tu per tu,
Si vedrà, fi vedrà chi ne può più.

Son buona buona
Fino a un tal fegno ;
Ma fe m' accendo,
Ma fe mi fdegno,
Quella pettegola
Farò tremar.
Lei fi vorrebbe
Metter con me ?
Ah ! mi fà ridere !
Povera femplice !
Quefto gran merito
In lei non v' è.
Se un' altra volta
Vuol provocarmi ;

Saprà

Saprò rifarmi,
Saprò parlar.
Quella pettegola
Farò tremar.

SCENA IV.

Contrappunto, poi Pascasio.

Con. Ha ragione da vendere.　Ora è d' uopo
　A Pascasio con qualche b　　terra
　Nascondere il desio della　　　　　

Paſ. Oh! che boccone amaro!　　　　　
　Di Timitilla il cor mi costa caro!

Con. Signor Pascasio, servo suo.　Che c' è?
　Voi mi parete affè molto turbato.

Paſ. Ahimè! mi ha Timitilla affassinato!
　Mi canzona senza altro.　**Con.** Eh! che di donne
　Ne potrete trovare una tempesta.

Paſ. Altre adesso non cerco, ed amo questa.

Con. Tal sia di voi: ma pur vo' consolarvi;
　E col cuor sulle labbra io vo' parlarvi.

Paſ. Non farà poco in vero,
　Se trovo un' uomo, che abbia il cor sincero.

Con. In una orecchia lo dirò.　Le donne—
　C' è nessun che ci ascolti? Nò: siam soli.
　Le donne, e stò per dire tutte quante
　Anno gusto d' aver più d' un' amante.
　Timitilla è così.　**Paſ.** Ma con me nò.
　Non m' ingarbuglia, oibò.　Mi raccomando
　A voi, mio Contrappunto, ed a Serpilla
　Di spiar Timitilla.
　Ma con ogni attenzione,
　Se segue a civettar con Don Sabbione;
　E farmene rapporto.

　　　　　　　　　　　　　　　　Con.

know how to talk to her, I'll make
that impudent huffey tremble.

S C E N A IV.

Contrappunto, afterwards Pafcafio.

*Con. She is quite in the right. Now I must conceal
my defire of revenge from Pafcafio, with some fine
story.*

*Paf. O what a bitter morfel! Timitilla's heart cofts
me dear.*

*Con. Mr. Pafcafio, your fervant, what is the matter?
Faith you feem much difturbed.*

*Paf. Alas! Timitilla has killed me. She certainly
plays the fool with me.*

Con. Oh you may find women enough.

*Paf. I am not now looking for others, for I am in love
with her.*

*Con. So let it be; but yet I am for comforting you,
and fpeak with the utmoft fincerity.*

*Paf. In good truth it is a great thing, to find a man
with a fincere heart.*

*Con. I'll whifper a word in your ear. The women in
general—is there no one liftening? No, we are
alone. The women in general, and I may venture
to fay all of them, are fond of having a multitude
of lovers, Timitilla is one of thofe.*

*Paf. But that won't go down with me, fhe fhan't draw
me in, in that manner; no indeed: I defire you, dear
Contrappunto, with Serpilla, to watch Timitilla with
the greateft care, to fee if fhe continues to coquet with
Don. Sabbione, and bring me word.*

Con.

ACT II.

Con. *I assure you again, that you are in the wrong;
but yet, courteous Pascasio, I know not how to deny you. I have not forgotten your complaisance, and
the many civilities you have loaded me with both
at home and abroad; who then could be such a brute
as to refuse you such a trifle; I love your good nature, I am your humble servant; therefore I tell
you that I am going, and will shew myself as your
true friend.*

Amiable Pascasio, I am going, adieu;
oh! that pleasing face of yours is
formed so admirably, as to be the
index of the goodness of your heart.
(He does not see at all; how am I
laughing at him; what fine fun!)
My complaisant friend, I am much
obliged to you, I speak nothing but
truth, believe me.

SCENE V.

Pascasio solus.

*I place great confidence in Contrappunto. I am not
so foolish. Faith I would have Timitilla wholly
mine, and always mine; and that D. Sabsione
may not impose upon me, I will have all my eyes
about me. Matrimony is a kind of trade, that I
would not enter into partnership with others.*

Con. Io vi replico ancor che avete torto.
Ma, Pafcafio gentil, con tutto ciò,
Non vi sò dir di nò. Non ho fcordato
Quanto fiete garbato; e quanti onori
In voftra cafa, e fuori
M' avete fatto. E poi chi è quel brutale,
Che a voi ricufi bagatella tale?
Amo il voftro buon cuore.
Io vi fon fervitore. Onde vi dico,
Che vado, e che agirò da vero amico.

Pafcafio amabile,
Io parto, addiò,
Vi fon fervitor.
Ma quel bel volto
Sì ben raccolto
Spiega l' idea
Del fuo buon cuor.
[Pur non s' avvede
Che ora lo burlo :
Che gran piacer !]
Amico garbato !
Vi fono obbligato ;
Vi dico da vero,
Credetelo a me.

S C E N A V.

Pafcafio.

Di Contrappunto in ver mi fido, e molto;
Io non fono sì ftolto.
Timitilla alla fè
Voglio che tutta, e fempre fia per me.
E a fin che Don Sabbion non m' infinocchi,
Aprirò tanto d' occhj. Il matrimonio
E certa mercanzia,
Che non vo' far con altri in compagnia.

H

Son

the charming Serpilla, and none at all of Timitilla.
Well, patience, patience.

Ser. [*She begins with her accustomed rudeness.*]
Con. *I discharge my duty equally to both of you.*
Ti. *Oh, 'tis very evident. I wish you joy, Madam.*
Ser. *I congratulate you in my turn.*
Ti. *Very fine, Madam ?*
Ser. *Your ladyship enchants every body.*
Ti. *Your ladyship makes every body in love with you.*
Ser. *silly girl.*
Ti. *Foolish wench.*
Con. *Fie! hold your tongues! will you expose your-*
selves ?
Ser. *She begun first.*
Ti. *Fine again. Truth is a good thing ; but you op-*
pose my union with D. Sabbione.
Ser. *I am glad you know it.*
Ti. *What ? again ?*
Ser. *From the little you have seen, you may judge what*
is to come.
Con. *Hold, hold a little for heaven's sake, let us go*
on with our lesson. 'Tis your turn, Timitilla, come
this way, and sing.
Ser. [*Now there will be a fine discord.*]

Ti.   Think how to fix my charmer—
Con.   Think how to fix my charmer—
Ti.   Think how to fix my charmer.—

Ser. [*She cannot sing a single note, how it pleases*
me !]
Con. *If I know any thing of my art, here are three*
sharps.
Ti. *What is it to me if there were six ?*
Con. *Grant me patience. Let us begin again, come.*
Ser. [*The poor ignorant creature does not know where*
she is.]

                                        Ti.

Chiaro si vede che hà nitto l' impegno
Per la bella Serpilla,
Niente per Timitilla; e ben pazienza.
Ser. [Cominciam colla solita infolenza.]
Con. Fò il mio dovere con ugual premura.
Ti. Oh, il fatto l' afficura! Io bramerei
Rallegrarmi con lei.   *Ser.* Vo' fare anche io
Con lei l' obbligo mio.   *Ti.* Brava, Signora!
Ser. Ella ciafcuno incanta!   *Ti.* Ella innamora!
Ser. Frafchetta!   *Ti.* Pazzarella!   *Con.* Olà, tacete:
Far nafar vi volete?   *Ser.* Effa è la prima.
Ti. Oh, bravi ancor! La verità fi ftima!
Voi però con Sibbiun mi traverfate.—
Ser. Ho piacer lo fappiate.   *Ti.* Ancor di più?
Ser. Se poco è quel che fù,
Potete preveder quel che farà.
Con. Zitte, zitte, un pochin per carità.
Seguitiam la lezzione.
Tocca a voi, Timitilla,
Venite quà, cantate.
Ser. [Ora fi fentiran delle ftuonate!]

Ti.   *Penfa a ferbarmi, a caro—*
Con.   *Penfa a ferbarmi, a caro—*
Ti.   *Penfa a ferbarmi, a caro.—*

Ser. [Non ne dice una bota.   Oh, che piacere!]
Con. Se è vero il mio meftiere,
Tre diefis fon quefti agli occhj miei.
Ti. Che importa a me, fe foffero anche fei?
Con. Che pazienza! Torniam da capo, via.
Ser. [Non sà l' ignorantella ove fi fia.]

G   *Ti.*

Ti. *Penſa a ſerbarmi, o cara,*
I dolci affetti tuoi——

Con. Oibò! Queſto è un gran fallo.
Queſto è un ſpropoſitaccio da cavallo.

Ti. Coſa dire volete?

Con. Che voi ſtuonate maledettamente.

Ti. Andate via ; non ne ſapete niente.
Io ne ſò più di voi. Che? voi ridete?
Ora mi ſentirete ;
Quì, quì, ſul voſtro viſo
Voglio un' aria cantare all' improviſo.
Io ſon quella che ſono : e ogni un mi loda.

Ser. [Virtuoſa da vero a tutta moda.]

Ti. *Vedo ben, che voi volete*
Un po' troppo alzar la teſta ;
Ma ſignore mio garbato, [a Contrappunto.
Bel viſino delicato, [a Serpilla.
La mi ſcuſi, la mi' intenda,
Favoriſca, non ſi offenda ;
Cari, cari, ſoggettini,
Proverete, ſentirete,
Quel che penſo, e che ſò far.
Come due pulcin bagnati,
Zitti, zitti, ſpennacchiati,
Reſterete chini, chini
Il mio garbo ad ammirar.

Ser. Ben? colla voſtra flemma? avete udito?

Con. Ah, me la lego al dito! Ser. Ah! queſta volta
Non vo' che l'ira mia reſti ſepolta.

Con. Sepolta non ſtarà. Cara Serpilla,
Già la mia mente ſtilla
Di vendicarci il modo. Ser. E quando? Con.
Adeſſo.

Ser. Gli affronti, che ci ſà, vanno all' eceſſo.

Con.

Ti.   Think how to fix, my charmer thy
dearest dearest love.

Con. Fie, fie, this is very bad, it is a shameful error
Ti. What do you mean?
Con. That you make a confounded discord.
Ti. Get you gone, you know nothing of the matter. I
know more than you. What? do you laugh? You
shall hear me immediately, upon the spot, sing an air
extempore. I know what I am myself, and I have
the esteem of every one.
Ser. She is a true fashionable singing girl.

Ti.   I very well perceive that you have a mind to
hold up your heads a little too high, but my
very good Sir, [*to Contrappunto.*] my modest
pretty face, [*to Serpilla.*] Be so kind as to listen
to me, and pray don't be offended, my dear
Sir, my dear madam, you shall find to your cost,
what I design to do. Like two little chickens
bemired and stript of their feathers, you shall be
silenced and humbled, envying my prosperity.

Ser. Well, Mr. Patience, did you hear her?
Con. Oh, I'll set it down in my book.
Ser. I will not now keep my anger within bounds.
Con. There is no occasion. My dear Serpilla, I am
now hatching the means of revenge.
Ser. But when?
Con. Immediately.
Ser. The affronts which we receive are intolerable.

Con.

Con. See the old man is coming: get away.

Ser. No, I'll help you, rail against her.

Con. 'Tis not proper now. Get you gone; but farther, I beg you, if you happen to meet Timitilla, that you would diffemble your anger.

Ser. Nay, if I fall into her company, and muft not let a word drop against her, it will certainly chóak me.

Con. Confider, I am affronted as well as you, follow my advice. Do you underftand me? you have a fpirit fit for any thing; have your wits about you.

Ser. The more I think of it, the more I am enraged; I don't know what this foolifh girl means, fhe will not only have her drove of lovers; but what is worfe, even under my nofe will fhe be playing, dancing, and finging with a thoufand gallants, and fpitefully pluming herfelf and flaunting. Oh but if I am put in a paffion, you fhall fee fome fine fport, when we are oppofed to each'other, it will foon be known which of us is the more able,

I am good natured to a certain pitch; but if I am provoked, I'll make that impudent huffey tremble. Will fhe put herfelf in competition with me? Ha, ha, it makes me laugh. Poor fimpleton! No, fhe has not fo much merit. If fhe fhould provoke me again, I fhall know how to revenge myfelf, I fhall

know

Con. Ecco il vecchio che vien : partite.. *Ser.* Nò:
A dir mal di colei v' aiuterò.

Con. Or non è tempo : andate : anzi vi prego,
Se Timirilla mai voi rincontrate,
L' ira diffimulate. *Ser.* Oh! se là trovo,
E scappar non mi deve una parola,
Son certa, mi verrà tanto di gola.

Con. Penfate, che ancor io fono l' offefo :
Seguite il mio configlio. Avete intefo?
Voi fiete un fpiritello,
Che di tutto sà far. State in cervello.

Ser. Più ch ci penfo, più mi vien la rabbia.
Non sò che cofa s' abbia quefta frafca-
Non fol gli amanti vuole uno per tafca;
Ma quel ch' è peggio ancor; fugli occhj miei
Con mille cicifbei,
Se fuona, balla, o canta,
Si pavoneggia alle mie fpalle, e vanta.
Ah! fe mi falta al fin la mofca al nafo,
Vo' fi veda un bel cafo. A tu per tu,
Si vedrà, fi vedrà chi ne può più.

Son buona buona
Fino a un tal fegno;
Ma fe m' accendo,
Ma fe mi fdegno,
Quella pettegola
Farò tremar.
Lei fi vorrebbe
Metter con me?
Ah! mi fà ridere!
Povera femplice!
Quefto gran merito
In lei non v' è.
Se un' altra volta
Vuòl provocarmi;

Saprà

Saprò rifarmi,
Saprò parlar.
Quella pettegola
Farò tremar.

SCENA IV.

Contrappunto, poi Pascasio.

Con. Ha ragione da vendere. Ora è d' uopo
A Pascasio con qualche bagatellora
Nascondere il defia della ....

Pas. Oh! che boccone amaro!
Di Timitilla il cor mi costa caro!

Con. Signor Pascasio, servo suo. Che c' è?
Voi mi parete affè molto turbato.

Pas. Ahimè! mi ha Timitilla affassinato!
Mi canzona senza altro. *Con.* Eh! che di donne
Ne potrete trovare una tempesta.

Pas. Altre adesso non cerco, ed amo questa.

Con. Tal sia di voi: ma pur vo' consolarvi;
E col cuor sulle labbra io vo' parlarvi.

Pas. Non sarà poco in vero,
Se trovo un' uomo, che abbia il cor sincero.

Con. In una orecchia lo dirò. Le donne—
C' è nessun che ci ascolti? Nò: siam soli.
Le donne, e stò per dire tutte quante
Anno gusto d' aver più d' un' amante.
Timitilla è così. *Pas.* Ma con me nò.
Non m' ingarbuglia, oibò. Mi raccomando
A voi, mio Contrappunto, ed a Serpilla
Di spiar Timitilla.
Ma con ogni attenzione,
Se segue a civettar con Don Sabbione,
E farmene rapporto.

Con.

know how to talk to her, I'll make
that impudent hussey tremble.

S C E N A IV.

Contrappunto, afterwards Pascasio.

Con. *She is quite in the right. Now I must conceal my desire of revenge from Pascasio, with some fine story.*

Pas. *O what a bitter morsel! Timitilla's heart costs me dear.*

Con. *Mr. Pascasio, your servant, what is the matter? Faith you seem much disturbed.*

Pas. *Alas! Timitilla has killed me. She certainly plays the fool with me.*

Con. *Oh you may find women enough.*

Pas. *I am not now looking for others, for I am in love with her.*

Con. *So let it be; but yet I am for comforting you, and speak with the utmost sincerity.*

Pas. *In good truth it is a great thing, to find a man with a sincere heart.*

Con. *I'll whisper a word in your ear. The women in general—is there no one listening? No, we are alone. The women in general, and I may venture to say all of them, are fond of having a multitude of lovers, Timitilla is one of those.*

Pas. *But that won't go down with me, she shan't draw me in, in that manner; no indeed: I desire you, dear Contrappunto, with Serpilla, to watch Timitilla with the greatest care, to see if she continues to coquet with Don. Sabbione, and bring me word.*

Con.

*Con. I assure you again, that you are in the wrong;
but yet, courteous Pascasio, I know not how to deny you; I have not forgotten your complaisance, and
the many civilities you have loaded me with both
as home and abroad; who then could be such a brute
as to refuse you such a trifle; I love your good nature, I am your humble servant; therefore I tell
you that I am going, and will shew myself as your
true friend.*

Amiable Pascasio, I am going, adieu;
oh! that pleasing face of yours is
formed so admirably, as to be the
index of the goodness of your heart.
(He does not see at all; how am I
laughing at him; what fine fun!)
My complaisant friend, I am much
obliged to you, I speak nothing but
truth, believe me.

SCENE V.

Pascasio solus.

*I place great confidence in Contrappunto. I am not
so foolish. Faith I would have Timislila wholly
mine, and always mine; and that D. Sablsone
may not impose upon me, I will have all my eyes
about me. Matrimony is a kind of trade, that I
would not enter into partnership with others.*

I am

Con. Io vi replico ancor che avete torto.
Ma, Pascasio gentil, con tutto ciò,
Non vi sò dir di nò. Non ho scordato
Quanto siete garbato; e quanti onori
In vostra casa, e fuori
M' avete fatto. E poi chi è quel **brutale,**
Che a voi ricusi bagatella tale?
Amo il vostro buon cuore.
Io vi son servitore. Onde vi dico,
Che vado, e che agirò da vero amico.

     Pascasio amabile,
     Io parto, addio,
     Vi son servitor.
     Ma quel bel volto
     Sì ben raccolto
     Spiega l' idea
     Del suo buon cuor.
     [Pur non s' avvede
     Che ora lo burlo:
     Che gran piacer!]
     Amico garbato!
     Vi sono obbligato;
     Vi dico da vero,
     Credetelo a me.

SCENA V.

Pascasio.

Di Contrappunto in ver mi fido, e molto.
Io non sono sì stolto.
Timitilla alla fè
Voglio che tutta, e sempre sia per me.
E a fin che Don Sabbion non m' infinocchi,
Aprirò tanto d' occhj. Il matrimonio
È certa mercanzia,
Che non vo' far con altri in compagnia.

H   *Son*

ATTO II.

Son vecchio, è certo;
Ma sono esperto,
E di quei cesso
Io me la beffo:
Faccia che vuole,
Che trovi cabale,
Che tenda trappole,
Che faccia imbrogli,
Metta scompigli,
Io me la rido;
In due parole,
Non me la fà.

SCENA VI.

Anticamera in casa di Pascasio.

Don Sabbione in collera, e Timitillo che tenta placarlo.

D. S. **Non** vo' sentire, e non mi sò dar pace.
Ti. Fermatevi. D. S. Mendace!
Ti. Ma sentite. D. S. Non deggio.
Ti. Via, Don Sabbion. D. S. Più che pregate, è
    peggio.
Ti. Son fida. D. S. Non lo credo.
    Scuse non voglio quando sento e vedo.
Ti. Semplice lazzo fù.
D. S. Non me ne dite più.
    Levatevi di quà.
Ti. Oh Dio! che crudeltà!
    Ancor mi discacciate?
D. S. Vi torno a replicar, andate, andate.
Ti. Ah, Don Sabbion, voi solo, sì, voi solo,
    Amo con cor sincero.

I am old, 'tis true, but I have a good
deal of experience; and as for that
monkey, I hold him in contempt. Let
him do what he will, let him cabal as
he pleases, let him set his engines, let
him intrigue, let him make riots, I
laugh at all. In a word, he shall do
nothing with me.

SCENE VI.

An antichamber in Pascasio's house.

*D. Sabbione in a passion, and Timitilla endeavour-
ing to appease him.*

D. S. I won't hear you, yet I know not how to be
easy.

Ti. Stop.

D. S. Lyar.

Ti. Do but hear.

D. S. I must not.

Ti. I beseech you, D. Sabbione.

D. S. The more you beseech, the worse it will be.

Ti. I am faithful.

D. S. I don't believe you, I don't want excuses that
contradict the evidence of my senses.

Ti. It was but in jest.

D. S. Say no more. Leave me.

Ti. Good God! what cruelty! do you banish me still?

D. S. I repeat again, be gone, be gone.

Ti. Ah, D. Sabbione, 'tis you, alone you alone, that I
love with sincerity.

H 2   D. S.

D. S. *Your story is tedious: there is no truth in what you say.*

Ti. *But this is downright tyranny.*

D. S. *Your very humble servant.*

Ti. *Behold me at your feet.*

D. S. *Deceitful woman!* (*Alas! what do I see?*)

Ti. *Mercy.*

D. S. *Does she ask mercy, who has no regard to fidelity.* (*Alas! I am moved.*)

Ti. *Here I am entirely yours.*

D. S. (*I can bear it no longer.*)

Ti. *What can I do more?*

D. S. *Come, arise.*

Ti. *Have compassion.*

D. S. (*In truth she sets me all on fire.*)

Ti. *If you forsake me, I shall die with despair.*

D. S. *It is your own fault.*

Ti. *Alas! what torment! what sorrow!*

D. S. *You deceive me, I know.*

Ti. *If you don't believe me, it will kill me.*

Ah cruel man! will you make me weep?
I will weep and sob. See, see how
red my eyes are now; well, come,
what do you stay for? Turn your face,
smile upon me. Come nearer this
way, have compassion.

SCENE VII.

Don Sabbione *solus.*

O women, women! ye stars! ye heavens! ye gods! how she has disturbed me! I feel——what do I feel?

D. S. È lunga la canzon! nò, non è vero.
Ti. Ma quella è tirannia!
D. S. Io sono schiavo di vossignoria.
Ti. Eccomi a' vostri piedi. *D. S.* Ingannatrice!
　　[Che vedo? ohimè!] *Ti.* Pietà! *D. S.* Pietà
　　mi chiede
　　Chi non sà che sia fede. [Ah, son commos-
　　　so!]
Ti. Son quì tutta per voi. *D. S.* [Durar non pos-
　　　so!]
Ti. Che deggio far di più?
D. S. Levatevi, via, su.
Ti. Abbiate compassione.
D. S. [Mi si scalda da ver tutto il polmone.]
Ti. Se voi m' abbandonate,
　　Morirò disperata. *D. S.* Vostro danno.
Ti. Ahi, che dolor! che affanno!
D. S. M' ingannate, lo sò.
Ti. Se voi non mi credete, io morirò.

Ah, crudel! vuoi tu che io pianga?
Singhiozzando piangerò.
Guarda, guarda questi occhietti
Come rossi ora gli fò.
Basta, via, che cosa aspetti?
Volta il viso—fà un sorriso—
Falti in quà—abbi pietà.

SCENA VII.

Don Sabbione.

Oh, donne! oh, donne! oh, stelle! oh, cieli!
　　oh, Dei!
M' ha commosso costei!

3　　　　　　　　　Mi

Mi fento—e che mi fento? Io non lo sò.
Vorrei—dovrei—potrei—ma oibò, oibò.
Ella mi porta amor ; la poverina!
Per me piange, e fofpira.
Or guarda un poco—e poi con il tutore
La vidi far l' amore.
Che rifolvo ? che fò ? Sono imbrogliato!
Se afcolto l' amor mio,
Placato già fono io.
Se Pafcalio rammento,
Tutto per gelofia tremar mi fento.
Sì, voglio andar—ma nò—chi sà—fe poi—
Quel pianto—forfe adeffo—oh, cafo orrendo!
Parlo—dico—difdico—e non m' intendo.

*Per l' affanno, in cui mi veggo,
Dove fon ? che fò ? non fò.
Non hò fiato : in più non regge :
Freddo ftò : già vengo meno :
Batte il polfo : e tutto in feno
Palpitando il cor mi và :
Batte, batte : oh che pietà!*

SCENA VIII.

Lindoro e Rofmira.

Lin. 'E partito : entriam pur. Come dicevo,
Contrappunto, e Serpilla
Son contro Timitilla ; e non han torto.
Rof. Anche io mal volentieri la fopporto ;
E in quel che fan gli fcufo.
Ma più prefto conclufo
Credo ben che farebbe il noftro nodo ;

feel? I know not: I would---I should---I could---
No, no. She offers me her affections, poor girl!
for me she weeps and sighs. Now let us consider a
little---I saw her making love to her guardian.
What shall I resolve upon? what shall I do? I am
all confusion: if I hearken to my love, I am already
appeased: if again I think of Pascasio, I tremble
all over with jealousy. Well, I'll go---no it can't
be---who knows---but if----those tears----perhaps
now---oh horrible! I talk---I say---and unsay---
and know not what I should be at.

> Through the grief in which I find myself, I
> know not where I am, or what I am do-
> ing: I lose my breath, I cannot stand
> upon my feet: I grow cold, and I faint:
> My pulses beat, and my heart is ready to
> leap out of my bosom; it beats, it beats:
> what a sad thing it is!

SCENE VIII.

Lindoro and Rosmira.

Lin. He is gone, so let us go in---As I was saying
Contrappunto and Serpilla are against Timitilla,
and not without reason.

Rof. And I too can hardly bear her, or excuse her, and
her lover's behaviour. But I firmly believe that
our marriage will be sooner compleated, if means
could

could be found for her espousing D. Sabbione: from whence the opposition—

Lin. *I don't deny it: but I would have you think, that nothing in the world can hurt our wedding.*

Rof. *Well then, since it is so, let them go on as they please.*

Lin. *I'll stay here no longer; for as Pascasio is smelling into every thing, and is ignorant of our loves, 'tis better for me to go to avoid suspicion.* [Exit.

Rof. *Let every one do as they please. As for me, it is sufficient that Lindoro preserve his faith, and love me as sincerely as I adore him.*

Is there a greater happiness in life? I am close to my dearest: I languish with love; and moreover, I dare to tell him, it is for you I languish.

S C E N E   IX.

A garden belonging to Pascasio.

Timitilla, and D. Sabbione, then Serpilla, and Contrappunto on one side; afterwards Pascasio.

Ti. *Well, D. Sabbione, well, peace is made.*

D. S. *I am sorry for what is past.*

Ser. *(See, they are there.)*

Con. *Listen, we shall discover their thoughts.*

Ti. *It seems an age, till I get away.*

Con. *(Be quiet, and hark.)*

D. S. *I have stolen the keys of the doors.*

Se

Se fi trovaffe il modo,
Ch' ella da ver fpofaffe Don Sabbione.
Onde l' oppofizione—*Lin.* Anche io no'l nego,
Ma a credere vi prego,
Che neppure per ombra un pregiudizio
Potrà foffrire il noftro fpofalizio.
Rof. Dunque lafciamgli far quando è così.
Lin. Non vo' più reftar quì. Giacche Pafcafio
Fiuta per tutto; e ignora il noftro aff-tto,
Meglio è che io parta per non dar fofpetto.
                                        [*Parte.*
Rof. Faccia ciafcun quel che gli piàce. A me
Bafta che la fua fè ferbi Lindoro,
E che m' ami fedel quanto io l' adoro.

Frà tutti i contenti
V' è gioia maggiore?
Son preffo al mio bene,
Sofpiro d' amore;
E dirgli ancor ofo
Sofpiro per te.

S C E N A   IX.

Giardino in cafa di Pafcafio.

Timitilla, e Don Sabbione, indi Serpilla, e Contrap-
punto in difparte; poi Pafcafio.

Ti. Sì, Don Sabbione, sì, fatta è la pace.
D. S. Quel ch' è ftato mi fpiace. *Ser.* [Eccogli quà.]
Con. [Attenti. Il lor penfier fi fcoprirà.]
Ti. Mi par mille anni di fcappar. *Ser.* [Udite?]
Con. [State zitta, e fentite.]
D S. Le chiavi delle porte già rubbai.

J   *Ser.*

Ser. [Buono!] *Con.* [A tempo arrivai!]
D. S. Questo colpetto
    Si farà quando tutti sono a letto.
Ti. E burleremo a un tratto
    Serpilla, Contrappunto, e il vecchio matto.
Ser. [Ah, Pascasio venisse!]
Con. [Venga, o non venga; basta quel che disse.
    Avanti; alò.] *Ser.* Viva, signora mia!
Con. Bravo, vossignoria! *Ti.* Che pretendete?
D. S. Come c'entrate voi? cosa volete?
Ser. Ho veduto. *Con.* Ho sentito.
Ser. Pascasio lo saprà presto, e pulito.
Ti. Così potete dir? *Ser.* Niente di buono.
D. S. Dite quel che vi pare. *Ti.* Io son chi sono.

Ser. ⎱	*Sì, signora, di là sù*
Con. ⎰	*S'è sentito che quà giù*
	Con Sabbiane fortunato
	Si trattava di fuggir.
Ti.	*Che impostura! io sol parlai —*
	Cosa dite? come mai?
	Ah, mi fate inorridir?
D. S.	*Tiritilla è sposa mia,*
	E voi altri andate via;
	Son padron di quà venir.
Ti.	*Che vi pare?* D. S. *Non temete.*
Ser. ⎱ *Con.* ⎰	*Vogliam dirlo.* D. S. *Non m'importa.*
Ser. ⎱ *Con.* ⎰	*S'è sentito.* D. S. *Maledetti!*

    Son lo sposo. ⎱ Ser. ⎰ Con. *La sbagliate*

                        D. S.

Ser. *Good!*

Con. *I came in the Nick of Time.*

D. S. *We'll strike this stroke, when every body is a-bed.*

Ti. *And so make fools of Serpilla, Contrappunto, and the old dotard all together.*

Ser. [*I wish Pascasio was here.*]

Con. *Come, or not, it is sufficient, that we tell him. Hearkee holla.*

Ser. *I wish you joy, Madam.*

Con. *Well done, Sir.*

Ti. *What do you mean?*

D. S. *How came you in here? what do you want?*

Ser. *I have seen something.*

Con. *I have heard something.*

Ser. *Pascasio shall soon know the whole of it.*

Ti. *What can you tell him?*

Ser. *No good.*

D. S. *Tell him what you please.*

Ti. *I am not afraid of what you can tell.*

Ser. ⎱ It is whisper'd that there was a design to
Con. ⎰ run away from hence with the happy D. Sabbione.

Ti. What a falsehood! I only said what are you talking of? How can it be? Indeed you quite astonish me.

D. S. Timitilla is betrothed to me, so you may get you gone, and I am master of my own actions.

Ti. What think you?

D. S. Don't be afraid.

Ser. ⎱ We will tell it.
Con. ⎰   D. S. I don't care.

Ser. ⎱ It is whisper'd.
Con. ⎰   D. S. Confound you.

I am to marry her.   Ser. ⎱ You are mistaken.
                Con. ⎰

D. S. You shall see it. $\left.\begin{array}{l}Ser.\\Con.\end{array}\right\}$ You are deceived.

D. S. So it is. $\left.\begin{array}{l}Ser.\\Con.\end{array}\right\}$ I won't bear.

D. S. Confound you! oh what a torture!

Ti. I know nothing of the matter. $\left.\begin{array}{l}Ser.\\Con.\end{array}\right\}$ We do.

Ti. I faid. $\left.\begin{array}{l}Ser.\\Con.\end{array}\right\}$ You cannot conceal it.

Ti. I don't fear you. $\left\{\begin{array}{l}Ser.\\Con.\end{array}\right.$ Are you fo bold?

D. S. Ah confound your Tongues!
     I advife you to get off.

Ser. } What affurance! what impudence! well,
Con. } Pafcafio fhall know it.

D. S. Innocence knows no fear.

Ti. Your impudence muft have an end.

Paf. Unhappy me! what is the matter? Are you
     here? You wretch! Good God! How will this
     end?

Ti. O my guardian!

Con. That gentleman!

Ser. The little huzzy——

$\left.\begin{array}{l}D. S.\\Ti.\end{array}\right\}$ We were here $\left.\begin{array}{l}Ser.\\Con.\end{array}\right\}$ Ready to run away.

Ti. I know nothing of   *Ser.* } She is in love with
     the matter   *Con.* } him.

D. S. O confound you! $\left.\begin{array}{l}Ser.\\Con.\end{array}\right\}$ She was in his arms.

D. S. } 'Tis not   *Ser.* } I fay yes, and this here
Ti. } true.   *Con.* } is the gallant.

Paf. To run away? *Ser.* Yes Sir.

Paf. With Sabbione? *Con.* So it is.

Paf. What do you fay to it? *Ser.* Punifh her.

Paf. What do you think of it, *Con.* Lock her up.

D. S. Lo vedrete. Ser. Con. } V' ingannate.

D. S. L' è così. Ser. Con. } Non vo' sentir.

D. S. Maledetti! oh che martir!

Ti. Io non sò. Ser. Con. } Seppiamo noi.

Ti. Io parlai. Ser. Con. } Celar non puoi.

Ti. Non vi tema. Ser. Con. } Hai tanto ardir?

D. S. Ah, linguacce maledette?
Vi configlio di partir.

Ser. }
Con. } Oh, che ardita? che infolente?
Sì, Pafcafio lo faprà.

D. S. }
Ti. } Non paventa l' innocenza,
L' infolenza finirà.

Paf. Ah, mefchino! Ah, cofa è flato?
Quì ti trovo, difgraziato!
Giufto ciel! che mai farà?

Ti. Ah, Tutore!

Con. Quefto fignore!

Ser. La sfacciatella!

D. S. }
Ti. } Stavo quì. Ser. Con. } Per fcappar via.

Ti. Non sò niente. Ser. Con. } E innamorata.

D. S. Maledetti! Ser. Con. } Era abbracciata.

D. S. }
Ti. } Non è vero. Ser. Con. } Signor sì.

E l' amante è quefto quì.

Paf. Scappar via? Ser. Signor sì.

Paf. Con Sabbione? Con. Ella è così.

Paf. Che ne dite? Ser. Gaftigatela.

Paf. Che credete? Con. Rinferratela.

A. 4.

a 4.;   *Cosa pensa? che dirà?*
Pas.   *Donna infida! mascalzone!*
            Voi l' avrete a far con me.

Ser. }
Con. }   *Bravo, bravo.*   D. S. }
                             Ti.   } *Via, via.*

Pas.   *Timitilla, andate via.*
D. S.   *Anzi voglio che quì stia;*
            E di quà non anderà.

Ser. }
Con. }   *Che insolenza, padron mio!*

Pas.   *Insolente! temeraria!*

Ser. }
Con. }   *Questa quì la vo' goder.*

Pas.   *Via di quì.*   D. S. }
                           Ti.   } *Signor nò.*

Pas.   *Io commando, e così vo'.*

Ser. }
Con. }   *Bravo, bravo! me la rido.*

D. S. }
Ti.   }   *Via, tacete, disgraziati!*

D. S.   *Rispettate questa quì.*

Ser. }
Con. }   *Bravo, bravo! signor sì.*

Tutti.   *Oh, che rabbia, che ho nel petto!*
            Che dispetto, che mi fà!

Fine dell' Atto Secondo.

                                        A C T

All but *Pafcafio.* }	What can he think ? What can he fay to it ?
Paf.	Unfaithful woman! you rogue! I will be even with you both.
Ser. *Con.* }	Excellent, excellent. $\begin{array}{c} D. S. \\ Ti. \end{array}$ } Away, a- way.
Paf.	Timitilla retire.
D. S.	I will have her ftay, and not go from hence.
Ser. *Con.* }	What infolence is this, Sir!
Paf.	You are infolent, you are bold.
Ser. *Con.* }	This is good fport.
Paf.	Away from hence. $\begin{array}{c} D. S. \\ Ti. \end{array}$ } No, Sir.
Paf.	I command it, and will have it fo.
Ser. }	Excellent, excellent! fine fun!
D. S. *Ti:* }	Away, hold your tongues, ye wretches!
D. S.	Have fome refpect for the lady.
Ser. *Con.* }	Very well, very well: to be fure, Sir.
All.	How my bofom fwells with rage! how tormenting is this affair.

The End of the Second Act.

ATTO

ACT III.

SCENE I.

An Anti-chamber adjoining to Pafcafio's Garden.

Pafcafio, Contrappunto, Serpilla, Rofmira, and
Lindoro.

Paf. HERE, *quick, Contrappunto, call me a lock-*
fmith directly : for Don Sabbione has ftolen
my keys, and I must make faft all my windows large
and fmall, and all my doors great and little. [Exit.

Con. Get you gone. You are a wife one : you fhall foon
know what I am fifhing for, for Don Sabbione fhall
be the lockfmith ; the eafier to deceive him, we fix
are now all reconcil'd : 'Tis better certainly for us
to feparate, Serpilla, in order to fave appearances a
little.

Ser. Yes, yes, let us be fteady to our engagements, and
we fhall gain our point, and laugh in the old man's
teeth.

Rof. I will lofe no time ; but haften to my father, to
tell him of our loves, and I fhall fpeak to him roundly,
and plainly. [Exit.

Lin. if things are as I am informed, I fhall be happy
without much trouble.

Ye who fet you hearts upon beauty in
its native fimplicity, don't truft too
much

ATTO III.

SCENA I.

Anticamera contigua al giardino di Pascasio.

Pascasio, Contrappunto, Serpilla, Rosmira, e Liadoro.

Pas. SUBITO, Contrappunto,
Chiamatemi un magnano in questo punto.
Don Sabbione le chiavi mi rubbò,
Ed io chiuder farò
Finestre, finestroni, e finestrelle,
E le porte, e i portoni, e particelle.   [*Parte.*

Con. Vå pure: oh, tu stai fresco!
Quello che adesso pesco
In breve vederai.   Questo magnano
Don Sabbione farà.   Già per gabbarlo
La pace è fatta trà noi sei.   Serpilla,
Affin che l' apparenza un po' salviamo,
E' meglio certo che ci separiamo.

Ser. Sì, sì, passiamo a' fatti:
Stiam fermi a' nostri patti; e goderemo,
E alla barba del vecchio rideremo.

Ros. Anche io non perdo tempo.   Adesso al padre
Per dichiarare il nostro amor m' affretto;
E gli saprò parlare e tondo e netto   [*Parte.*

Lin. Se la cosa è così, come ogn' un dice,
Senza molto stentar farò felice.

*Voi che adorate il vanto
Di semplice beltà,*

K   *Non*

Non vi fidate tanto
Di chi tradir non sà ;
Che fortunato e grato
Sempre non è l' amor.

SCENA II.

Serpilla e Contrappunto.

Ser. Dell' ira di Pascasio, e del suo ceffo
    Ora sì, che da vero me ne beffo.
Con. Lasciamo andare il vecchio.
    Alle nozze, alle nozze m' apparecchio.
Ser. Certo questa è la vera,
    Tutti sei maritiamoci sta sera.
Con. Mi vo' presto spicciare,
    E concludere quel che s' ha da fare
    Perchè sento sul serio all' appetito
    D' esser vostro marito
    Mescolato nel core un certo affanno,
    Ed ogni ora, mio ben, mi pare un' anno.
Ser. Anche io son sì vogliosa
    D' essere vostra sposa,
    Che quando non vi vedo,
    Agli occhi miei non credo ;
    E sempre il cor mi dice eccolo eccolo ;
    Ed ogni ora, mio ben, mi pare un secolo.

    Fidi amanti, sventurati,
    Che languite, che penate,
    Invidiate il bel contento,
    Che io già sento nell' amar.

Grati

much to a pretended ignorance of
deceit, for love does not always meet
with a happy grateful return.

SCENE II.

Serpilla and Contrappunto.

Ser. Now indeed, I can truly laugh at Pafcafio's an-
ger, and his ugly face.
Con. No more of the old man. I am preparing for
the wedding, the wedding.
Ser. Certainly, that is the thing of things. We are
all fix of us to be married this evening.
Con. I will foon difpatch, and finifh what I have to
do: for, ferioufly, I find in my heart no lefs anxiety
than defire to be your bufband, and every hour, my
love, appears to me a year.
Ser. I too am fo defirous of being your wife, that
when I do not fee you, I don't believe my eyes, for
you always are prefent to my heart; and every hour,
my love, appears to me an age.

O ye faithful lovers, who are unhappy,
and languifh, and fuffer, envy the fweet
content which now I feel in love.

K 2   Agre-

O agreeable chains! O pleafing torments! I am united to my deareft, my amiable, charming hufband is coming to comfort my foul.

SCENE III.

Centrappunto folus.

Con. So it is ; thus the matter ftands when love is become mafter of one's heart ; farewell prudence. Every remedy is vain. It is a miracle to find one in an age that has not yielded to it ; and you fcarcely meet with one in a million. I know that a great philofopher thought he was right in maintaining, that love may be carried on with mere friendfhip ; but I would venture to lay any wager, that when a beautiful object warms any of our fancies, we fhould throw afide philofophy.

There is a current opinion, which makes thofe laugh that know any thing of the matter, that the difciples of Plato in making love do not exceed the bounds of friendfhip. What fay you? do you believe them? if a Platonift happens to be near a fine woman, what fay you? how would it end? Would not the philofopher catch fire by degrees.

SCENE

33

3

ATTO333 III.

Grati lacej! amate pene!
Son unita al caro bene!
L' amoroso dolce sposo
Vien questa alma a consolar.

SCENA III.

Contrappunto.

Con. Tanto è: là và così. Quando l'amore
Fatto è padron d'un core, addio riguardi;
Ogni rimedio è tardi. In una etade
L' incontrar chi non cade, è un gran por-
tento;
E se ne trova appena uno per cento.
Sò che un Filosofone
Crede d' aver ragione
Di sostenere che all' amor si fa
Per mera civiltà. Ma pur scommetto,
Che allor che un vago oggetto
Ci scalda a quanti siam la fantasia,
Mettiam da parte la filosofia.

Corre al mondo un' oppinione,
Che fà rider chi ne sà.
Che i scolari di Platone
Fan l' amor per civiltà.
Voi, che dite? gli credete?
Se si trova un Platoncino
Presso qualche bel visino,
Ah! che dite? come andrà?
Tutto fuoco a poco a poco
Il Filosofo farà.

SCENA

SCENA IV.

Galleria corrispondente a diverse camere in casa di Pascasio.

Pascasio, e Timillilla altercando.

Pas. Vieni., *Ti.* Dove? Vedrai ;
Nò, non mi scapperai. *Ti.* Con vostra pace
Farò quel che mi piace. *Pas.* In questa stanza
Entra, presto, ubbidisci. *Ti.* Olà, fermate.
Pascasio, udite. Or che non c' è riparo,
La maschera mi levo, e parlo chiaro.
Vo' sposar Don Sabbione, e voi detesto.
Pas. Così tratti con me? che modo e questo?
Là chiusa resterai
Finche mi sposerai. *Ti.* Siete pur sciocco !
E per farvi restar come un' allocco ;
Entro di questo passo :
Ma cadrà sopra voi tutto il fracasso.
Sì ; chiedermi pietà vi sentirò :
Io me ne burlerò. Più non vi credo :
Chi voi siete, or m' avvedo. I piagnisterj,
Le lusinghe, le smanie, e le moine,
Non conteranno più. Nella pignatta
Saprete quel che bolle a cosa fatta.

Non credo a' detti tuoi
Pur troppo menzogneri ;
Quei sguardi lusinghieri
Più non mi placeranno.
E se mi dirai bella,
E se mi dirai cara,

SCENE IV.

A gallery in Pafcafio's houfe, having feveral rooms
opening into it.

Pafcafio and Timitilla.

Paf. Come here.

Ti. Where ?

Paf. You fhall fee ; no, you fhan't efcape me.

Ti. With your leave, I'll do as I pleafe myfelf.

Paf. Get you into that room ; obey me.

*Ti. Blefs. me, ftop. Pafcafio, bear me. Now that
there is no remedy, I'll pull off the mafk, and fpeak
plainly. I will marry D. Sabbione, and you I abhor.*

*Paf. Do you deal thus with me ? What ufage is this ?
you fhall be locked up in that room, till you marry
me.*

*Ti. You are quite a blockhead ! And to fhew what an
afs you are, I'll go in quietly, but you fhall fuffer
for it ; yes, I fhall hear you begging for mercy,
and I fhall laugh at you : I fhall truft you no more
now that I fee your difpofition : your tears, your
flatterings, your complaints, and fawnings, will all
be loft upon me. You fhan't know what is doing,
till all is over.*

I fhall no more truft your too deceitful
words ; your flattering looks fhall
no more appeafe my anger ; and if
you call me handfome, if you call
me deaf, I fhall no more believe
you ;

you; and I hope to fee you at my feet, all trembling and pale, afking me pardon.

SCENE V.

Pafcafio, then D. Sabbione as a lockfmith, afterwards Timitilla at the lattice of the chamber-door, where fhe is fhut up.

Paf. Get you in, there you are faft, and there ftay: keys, bars, chains, and bolts, fhall be employed to keep you in.

D. S. Your fervant, mafter.

Paf. Oh your fervant, I want to have all the locks of thefe doors changed directly; and you muft be quick in your work, and make it neat and ftrong.

D. S. It fhall be done; I fhall want a little oil.

Paf. You fhall have it prefently.

Ti. D. Sabbione?

D. S. O my jewel! are you here?

Ti. See where he has locked me up.

D. S. Have a little patience, my charmer, I'll come to releafe you in few minutes: we have all laid our heads together to deceive the old fool.

Ti. Hufh, my guardian, go afide.

D. S. Pleafe your honour, I am here.

Paf. Here is the oil.

D. S. I thank you, Sir.

Paf. Come, quick, difpatch.

D. S. Depend upon it, I'll foon have done.

Paf. I leave you here, but will be back in a moment.

D. S. If you pleafe, Sir, and in the mean while I'll work

[Pafcafio withdraws, and afterwards comes back.

This

Non ti darò più fede :
E spero che al mio piede
Verrai tremante e pallido
Perdono a domandar.

S C E N A V.

Pafcafio, poi Don Sabbione da Magnano, indi Timililla
dal cancello della camera, ove è chiufa.

Paf. Và pure: ci fei dentro ; e dentrò ftacci.
Chiavi, funi, catene, catenacci
Ti fapranno guardar. *D. S.* Servo, padrone.
Paf. Ti faluto. Mutar tutte vogl' io
Le ferrature adeffo a quefte porte ;
E fia pronto il lavoro, e proprio, e forte.
D. S. Servitù refterà. D'un poco d'olio
Avrei bifogno. *Paf.* Adeffo. *Ti.* Don Sab-
bione ?
D. S. Oh, gioia mia ! qui ftai ?
Ti. Vedi, dove m' ha chiusa ?
D. S. Sopporta, idolo mio. Frà pochi iftanti
Ad aprirti verrò. Tutti d' accordo
Già fiam per ingannar quefto balordo.
Ti. Zitto ; il rutor : và in là.
D. S. Luftriffimo, fon quà.
Paf. Ecco l' olio. *D. S.* Obbligato. *Paf.* Orsù,
fà prefto.
D. S. Non dubiti : fon lefto.
Paf. Ti lafcio : ma trà poco tornerò.
D. S. Lei vada pure : ed io lavorerò.
　　　　　[*Pafcafio fi ritira, e poi ritorna.*

Moglie vuol questo vecchio impazzito;
Timitilla però non farà.
Io di quella voglio esser màrito,
E lui crepi, se ben non gli và.
`E geloso nel fare all' amore:
Poverello! si sente un martello,
Tuppe, tuppe, tuppe nel seno;
Tuppe, tuppe, tuppe nel core;
Che penar giorno e notte lo fà;
Tuppe, tuppete, e tappetatà.

Paf. Bravissimo! che voce; che cantare!
D. S. Cantuzzando così mi svario un poco.
Paf. Fai bene: e questa serratura hai posta
    A maraviglia! A noi: mettiamo l'altra.
D. S. Or volando la servo.
    Ih! che bella figlia stà quì serrata!
Ti. Per la sua crudeltà!
D. S. Signor, mi fà pietà!
Paf. Và dentro, fraschettaccia:
    E tu segui il lavoro.
D. S. Sì, signore; mi sbrigo con due botte;
    Conciossiacosache sì fà già notte.

    Tuppe, tuppe, tuppe nel seno,
    Tuppe, tuppe, tuppe nel core;
    Che penar giorno e notte lo fà;
    Tuppe, tuppete, e tappatatà.

SCENA VI.

Don Sabbione, e Pascasio, indi Timitilla, poi Ros-
mira.

D. S. Ella è servita. *Paf.* Ebben. diman mattina
    A pagarti verrò. *D. S.* Mi maraviglio.
                          Paf.

This foolish old fellow wants a wife, but it shan't be Timitilla: I will be her husband; and if he don't like it, he may go hang himself. He is jealous in his love, poor wretch! he feels a hammer thump, thump, thump, in his bosom; thump, thump, thump against his heart, which makes him suffer night and day, thump, thump, thumpaty thump.

Paf. Excellent indeed! what a charming voice! what a fine finger!

D. S. I divert myself a little sometimes with humming.

Paf. You are in the right on't: you have put on this lock admirably well; come put on the other,

D. S. I fly to serve you. Lack-a-day! what a pretty girl is locked up here.

Ti. Thro' his cruelty.

D. S. Sir, she moves my compassion.

Paf. Get in you baggage, and you go on with your work.

D. S. Yes, Sir: I shall have done in a stroke or two, for it is growing late.

Thump, thump, thump in his bosom,
Thump, thump, thump in his heart,
Which makes him suffer night and day,
Thump, thumpaty, thumpaty, thump.

SCENE VI.

D. Sabbione and Pascasio, afterwards Timitilla, and last of all Rosmira.

D. S. Sir, your work is done.

Paf. Well; to-morrow morning I'll come and pay you.

D. S. Don't mention it.

Paſ. *I thank you, on my word, you are a clever 'fellow.*

D.S. *Sir, I take my leave, I am your moſt humble ſervant.* [Exit.

Paſ. *She ſeems to be crying. So, ſo, let us ſee what is the matter with her: I'll go with good nature, perhaps ſhe will yield; come hither Timitilla.*

Ti. *What are you wanting now? make haſte, be ſhort.*

Paſ. *How haughty! do you deſire my death?*

Ti. *What I have ſaid, I have ſaid, and I give myſelf no concern about you.*

Paſ. *What? is there no remedy?*

Ti. *No, no, I tell you.*

Paſ. *You will then make me your enemy, ſince you abuſe my good nature: I'll keep you in my chamber under lock and key. Come, walk along.*

Ti. *No, I'll ſtay here.*

Paſ. *Come, I tell you, get in.*

Ti. *Oh my arm——what are you doing?*

Paſ. *You ſhall ſuffer much worſe by and by, quick, quick, go in, I am not now afraid that ſhe ſhould eſcape me.*

[He locks her up in a room oppoſite to the firſt.

Roſ. *Papa an affair of great conſequence makes me wait upon you.*

Paſ. *For God's ſake get you gone, we'll talk another time.*

Roſ. *Mr. Lindoro aſks me in marriage.*

Paſ. *But you are to have D. Sabbione.*

Roſ. *You know already that he does not pleaſe me; nay, he has refuſed me.*

Paſ. *Be contented.*

Roſ. *Be contented?*

Paſ. *Oh, how tedious and tireſome your ſtory is! you have almoſt turned my head.*

[Exit.

Roſ.

Paſ. Io ti ringrazio: và, che ſei pur bravo.

D. S. Padron: la riveriſco ; e gli ſon ſchiavo. [*Parte.*

Paſ. Par ch' ella gridi. Oh, oh ! vediam coſa ha.
Colle buone anderò ; forſe cadrà.
Vien quà, mia Timitilla. *Ti.* Or che bramate ?
Sbrigatevi : alle corte.

Paſ. [Che ſuperba!] Volete la mia morte ?

Ti. Quel che v' ho detto, ho detto ;
Ed in pena per voi, nò, non mi metto

Paſ. E rimedio non c' è ? *Ti.* Nò, nò, vi dico.

Paſ. Dunque m' avrai nemico.
Giacchè t' abbuſi d' ogni corteſia,
Ti terrò ſotto chiave in ſtanza mia.
Sù, sù, camina. *Ti.* Nò ; quì voglio ſtare.

Paſ. Animo ; dentro. *Ti.* Il braccio—ohimè! che
fate ?

Paſ. Peggio in breve ſarà. Via, preſto, entrate.
Or che mi ſcappi più non ho paura.
[*La ſerra nella ſtanza oppoſta alla prima.*

Roſ. Signor l'adre, un' affar di gran premura
Mi conduce da voi.

Paſ. Di grazia andate ; e parleremo poi.

Roſ. Il cavalier Lindoro.
Mi chiede in ſpoſa. *Paſ.* E Don Sabbione avrete.

Roſ. Informato già ſiete : a me non piace :
Ed ei mi ricusò. *Paſ.* Datevi pace.

Roſ. Darmi pace? *Paſ.* Oh, l' è lunga! oh, che
tempeſta!
M' avete fatto già tanto di teſta ! [*Parte.*

Ros. Così mi lascia ? Io pure me ne vò;
Ed or senza altre ciarle il sposerò.

> Unita al mio sposo
> Son lieta, e felice;
> Piacere, riposo,
> Sperare mi lice;
> Il genio, l' amore
> M' ispira così.

SCENA VII.

NOTTE.

Don Sabbione con lanterna, poi Pascasio, indi Timitilla
dal Cancello della Camera, ove è chiusa.

D. S.   *Oh, che tenebre ! oh, che orrore !*
        Niuno sento rifiatar.
        Ma tremar già sento il core;
        Come batte ! come sbatte !
        Il timor mi prende già.

Non si sente una mosca. Il mondo è quieto.
Or nascodiamo quì questa lanterna.
Piano, diascolo, piano.
Non facciamo rumore.
Quì Timitilla stà ; cerchiamo il buco.
Eccolo. *Pas.* Chi và là ? *D. S.* Caspita ! zitto !
La pupilla, e il tutore in compagnia !
Pigliamo la lanterna, e andiamo via.
Ti. Parmi sentir qualcuno. Don Sabbione ?
D. S. Timitilla, quì stai ?
Ti. Son quì. Ma ohimè ! Deh, chiudi lanterna !
Ecco il tutore. *D. S.* Oh, sorte maledetta !

                          Pas.

Rof. *Does be leave me thus ? then I'll go too, and now without any more words I'll marry my lover.* [Exit.

> United to my love, I feel joy and
> happinefs, now I may hope for
> pleafure and peace, fuch are the
> fuggeftions of love, and my good
> genius.

SCENE VII.

NIGHT.

Don Sabbione with a dark Lanthorn, then Pafcafio,
afterwards Timitilla from the Lattice of the Room,
where fhe is fhut up.

D. S.   Oh what an awful darknefs! I don't
hear a breath, Oh now I feel a
trembling in my heart : how it
throbs! how it beats! fear feiz,s
me all over.

*Not a moufe ftirs : every thing is bufht. Come I'll
bide the lanthorn here. The deuce! foftly, foftly,
this is Timitilla's chamber, now for the key-hole :
bere it is.*

Paf. *Who is there ?*

D. S. *How is this! ft : what the guardian and his
ward together! I'll take my lanthorn and get me
gone.*

Ti. *Methinks I bear fomebody. Don Sabbione ?*

D. S. *Dear Timitilla, are you there ?*

Ti. *I am here ; good God! pray fbut up the lanthorn ;
bere comes my guardian.*

D. S. *Accurfed accident !*

Paſ. *I heard a noiſe : who is there ? if any body ſtirs, I'll blow his brains out : no body moves ; may be it was the cat.*

D. S. *Miau, miau, miau, miau.*

Paſ. *I was right ; I take breath. It is certainly the cat.*

Ti. *My Life.*

D. S. *What ſay you ?*

Ti. *Open the door quickly.*

D. S. *I am coming.*

Ti. *Softly, the deuce ! my guardian !*

Paſ. *This is no cat, the door creaks. It muſt be thieves. Heavens ! the tinder is wet. I hear them breathe. Villains ! the door is opened ! confuſion !*

D. S. *Now let us lock him in.*

Ti. *Oh, do, do.*

Paſ. *What inſolence !*

Ti. *What tranſport !*

D. S. *What pleaſure !*

Ti. *Are you there ?*

D. S. *Then there you may ſtay.*

Ti. *The keys and bolts now fall to your lot.*

Paſ. *Open the door, or I'll.—*

Ti. *Will you conſent to my marrying Don Sabbione ?*

Paſ. *No perfidious woman, no.*

Ti. *Then ſtay in your cage.*

D. S. *Will you conſent to my marrying Timitilla ? and change your fury into compliance ?*

Paſ. *I'll never give my conſent.*

D. S. *Then ſtay in your cage.*

Paſ. *No, no I ſhan't ſtay here. Help, neighbours.*

D. S. *A little louder.*

Ti. *No one hears you.*

Paſ. *Ah you are all-combined to betray me I find, I'll get out of the window into the garden, oh, I'll have ſatiſfaction for this affront in a court of juſtice.*

[Exit.
Ti.

Paf. Rumor fentii. ‹ Chi è là ? Niuno fi muova,
     Chè l' avvampo di fuoco.
     Ma niun camina.   Sarà ftato il gatto.
D. S. Gnao, gnao, gnaragnagnao.
Paf. Non m' ingannai: refpiro : è certo il gatto.
Ti. Anima mia.   *D. S.* Che vuoi?   *Ti.* Aprini
     preſto.
D. S. Ecco.   *Ti.* Fà piano.   Diamine! il tutore!
Paf. Queſto gatto non è.   Stride la porta.
     Ladri fon certo.   Oh, numi l umida è l' efca.
     Vi fento refpirar.   Oh, ladri infami!
     Quì l' ufcio è aperto! Oh, corpo del gran
     mondo l ·
D. S. Or chiudiamolo dentro.   *Ti.* Dici bene.
Paf. Olà! che impertinenza l
Ti. Che guſto l *D. S.* Che piacer! *Ti.* Ci fei? *D. S.*
     Or ſtacci.
Ti. Or fon per voi le chiavi, e i catenacci.
Paf. Aprite queſta porta, o che altrimenti—
Ti. Per fpofo Don Sabbion volete che io abbia ?
Paf. Nò, perfida, non vo'.   *Ti.* Reſtate in gabbia.
D. S. Volete, che io mi fpofi Timitilla ?
     E cambiare in amor la voſtra rabbia ?
Paf. Mai v' acconfentirò.   *D. S.* Reſtate in gabbia.
Paf. Nò ¡ chè non ci ſtarò.   Soccorfo! gente l
D. S. Più forte.   *Ti.* Neſſun fente.   *Paf.* Ah! tutti
     uniti
     Siete a tradirmi, il sò.   Dalla fineſtra
     Ora mi calo nel giardino.   Ah l conto·
     In giuſtizia averò di queſto affronto. ¡ [*Parte*

M   *Ti.*

Ti. Vada dove gli pare. *D. S.* E vada dove
Non poſſa più tornare. Or noi contenti,
Dopo tanti tormenti,
Senza altro teſtimonio
Concludiam lietamente il matrimonio.

Ti. Non ho difficoltà.

D.S. Dammi la tua manina *Ti.* Eccola quà.

Occhj belli, troppo, troppo,
Jnfiammate queſto core:
Un tantino di pietà!

D. S.   *Occhj furbi, a poco a poco*
Vai bruciate queſto core;
Deh, partite in carità!

Ti.   *Non ho poſa.* *D.S.* *Andate in pace.*
Ti.   *Deh, ſcoſtatevi.* *D.S.* *Ecco quà.*
Ti.   *Ah, non tan—non tan—non tanto!*
Che mi fai già diſperar!

D.S.   *Ah, ſoſtie—ſoſtie—ſoſtiemmi!*
Io mi ſento liquefar!

Ti.   *Furbettino!* *D.S.* *Ladroncella!*
a. 2.   *Piano, piano, zitto, zitto,*
M' hai ſaputo innamorar.

SCENA Ultima.

Sala in Caſa di Paſcaſio.

Paſcaſio, Roſmira, Lindoro, Serpilla, Contrappunto,
poi Timitilla, e Don Sabbione per mano.

Paſ. Preſto, per carità, datemi un laccio;
Datemi un coltellaccio:
Quì, quì, voglio impiccarmi;
Quì, quì, ſugli occhj voſtri vo' ſcannarmi.

Lin. Si conſoli, ſignor. Lei sà chi ſono—

Roſ.

Ti. Go where you pleaſe.

*D. S. And go never to return. Let us now, being
at length made happy, after ſo many troubles conclude
our marriage joyfully without any farther ceremony.*

Ti. I have no objection.

D. S. Give me your dear hand:

Ti. Here 'tis.

Ye bright eyes, you let this heart too much
too much, on fire. Have a little mercy.

D. S. Ye roguiſh eyes, by little and little, you
conſume my heart: oh for heaven's ſake
get farther from me.

Ti. I have no reſt.

D. S. Go in peace.

Ti. Oh pray keep at a diſtance.

D. S. Then here I go.

Ti. Ah, nea—, nea—, ah nearer, or you'll
make me quite deſpair.

D. S. Ah, ſup—ah, ſup—ah, ſupport me! I feel
myſelf fainting.

Ti. You little rogue!

D. S. You little thief!

Both Softly, ſoftly, eaſy, eaſy, you have found
the way to catch my heart.

S C E N E the Laſt.

A Hall in Paſcaſio's Houſe.

Paſcaſio, Roſmira, Lindoro, Serpilla, Contrappunto,
afterwards Timitilla, and Don Sabione hand in
hand.

*Paſ. Quick, I beſeech you, give a rope, bring me ſome
old knife; I'll hang myſelf or cut my throat here before your eyes.*

Lin. Be of good heart, you know me—

Roſ.

Rof. *Forgive me, Papa.*

Paf. *There is no room for pardon, without my confent! execrable wretches!*

Ser. *Confent or not we are all married.*

Paf. *Where is Timitilla?*

Ti. *Here I invite you to my wedding.*

D. S. *Let all difturbances ceafe.*

Paf. *Oh miferable Pafcafio! what do I fuffer? the morfel is fnatched from my very mouth.*

Con. *Come, think no more on't.*

D. S. *Now let every one go to their own home.*

Con. *An excellent propofal! in fact to fpeak the truth, it would be a very difficult matter for three women to live together long in friendfhip.*

D. S. *Let's go. Brifk, come, let us be merry. Here's three weddings for you quite a-la-mode.*

Lin.	Reach me your hand my beautiful bride.
Rof.	I fhall be your happy bride, and always will be true.
Ti.	My guardian, to you I bow.
Paf.	O unhappy wretch!
D. S.	Ay there is no remedy, the thing is done.
Ti.	Pray take comfort, be of good heart.
Con. } *Ser.* }	Oh forgive us Sir.
Ti.	All is now over.
D. S.	I begin to be tired, for God's fake let us be going.
Ti.	True it grows late, health attend you.

Chorus. O Cupid, god of love, defcend,
     And clofely knit our faithful hearts.

Rof. Perdono, genitor. *Paf.* Non c'è perdono.
Senza il confenfo mio ? che fcellerati !
Ser. Confenfo, o non confenfo; fiàm fpofati.
Paf. Timitilla dov' è ? *Ti.* Son quì. V' invito
Alle mie nozze. *D.S.* E il chiaffo fia finito.
Paf. Oh, povero Pafcafio !
Cofa foffrir mi tocca !
Il boccon m' han levato dalla bocca !
Con. Via, non ci penfi più. *D. S.* Refta che vada
Ciafcun per la fua ftrada. *Con.* Oh, bravo!
in fatti,
Che s' amino tre donne lungamente
Trà lor con cor fincero,
E' difficile affai, per dire il vero.
D. S. Partiamo! allegri ! via ! che ciafcun goda !
Ecco tre matrimonj a tutta moda.

Lin.   *Porgetemi la deftra*
       Spofina mia vezzofa.
Rof.   *Sarò felice fpofa,*
       E fida ognor farò.
Ti.   *Tutore, a voi m' inchino.*
Paf.   *Oh, povero mefchino !*
D. S. *Nò, non ferve altro,*
       La cofa è fatta.
Ti.   *Vi prego a confolarvi,*
Con.) *E ftarvi di buon cor.*
Ser.) *Perdono a noi, fignore.*
Ti.   *Il tutto è già fpicciato.*
D. S. *Comincio ad annoiarmi,*
       Andiam per carità.
Ti.   *E vero, sì ; fà tardi ;*
       Reftate in fanità.

Tutti. *Scenda cupido,*
        Dio degli amori,
        Gli amanti cuori
        Venga a legar.

E

And may thofe pleafures know no end,
Thofe pleafures, which true love imparts.

F I N I S.

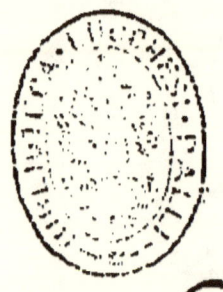